SARA TAKES ACTION

Sara took a deep breath to compose herself and faced them all.

"I've decided that I'm not going to leave until Aunt Hetty and Papa make up. Otherwise, I'll never be able to come back here."

Andrew shook his head. "You're leaving all right. You should have heard your father tonight."

"He was so mad at Aunt Hetty I thought his veins were gonna explode," Felix added dramatically.

"I don't care," flung out Sara in the face of this ominous fact. "I'm not leaving."

Felicity, who would have been shocked at such an idea only months ago, now found herself falling in readily with Sara.

"Well, we're going to have to disappear."

"Where do you suggest we hide you?" Andrew joked. "Under the bed?"

When Sara didn't even smile at this, they saw she was indeed serious. And if they didn't help her, who knew what trouble she'd get into on her own?

Also available in the Road to Avonlea series from Bantam Skylark books

Nothing Endures but Change

Storybook written by
Gail Hamilton

Based on the Sullivan Films Production
written by Heather Conkie
adapted from the novels of

Lucy Maud Montgomery

A BANTAM SKYLARK BOOK
NEW YORK · TORONTO · LONDON · SYDNEY · AUCKLAND

Based on the Sullivan Films Production produced by Sullivan Films Inc. in association with CBC and the Disney Channel with the participation of Telefilm Canada adapted from Lucy Maud Montgomery's novels.

Teleplay written by Heather Conkie
Copyright © 1989 by Sullivan Films Distribution, Inc.

This edition contains the complete text
of the original hardcover edition.
NOT ONE WORD HAS BEEN OMITTED.

RL 6, 008–012

NOTHING ENDURES BUT CHANGE

A Bantam Skylark Book / published by arrangement with
HarperCollins Publishers Ltd.

PUBLISHING HISTORY
HarperCollins edition published 1991
Bantam edition / February 1993

ISBN 0-553-48037-5

PRINTED IN THE UNITED STATES OF AMERICA

OPM   0 9 8 7 6 5 4 3 2 1

Nothing Endures but Change

Chapter One

Avonlea was a quiet village—and quiet villages naturally crave excitement. Even the smallest event, such as the passage of the regular transport coach, held promise, and today was no exception. Mrs. Potts and Mrs. Ray, two of the sharpest-tongued busybodies around, paused in the street as the heavy vehicle came rumbling through. The two liked to do their shopping at just about the time the coach was scheduled to arrive. They chewed over every scandal Avonlea had to offer, and lived in hopes that the coach might yield some juicy new morsel to add some variety to the usual gossip and speculation.

Usually their hopes were in vain. The coach rarely stopped. Hardly anyone at all ever got on or off, never mind someone interesting enough to stir up a commotion in Avonlea. That's why both women were quite taken by surprise when a hearty voice boomed out, "Stop here, driver," just as the coach drew abreast of them.

Obligingly, the coach clattered to a halt before the general store, which was pretty well in the center of the village. The door swung open. A handsome, extremely well-dressed gentleman in the prime of life stepped out, carrying a single valise.

"I prefer to walk the rest of the way, thank you," he called up to the driver, shutting the coach door with a thud.

His very voice carried an air of brisk command, proclaiming the arrival of a man of action, a man who wasted no time in getting what he wanted once he had made up his mind. The response was a deferential nod from the driver, who then drove off.

The passenger was left standing in the street, looking about him the way a man looks at a place he hasn't seen for a good many years. The expression on his face might have been called nostalgic, or it might have been called grim, depending on who was describing it. Shaking himself, he gripped his valise more tightly. With an unmistakable air of purpose, he headed out of sight down the road.

He hadn't noticed his two observers, but if he'd wanted to cause a stir, the effect he had upon the two women was everything a sensationalist could have desired. They stood stock-still, their mouths agape, until the man was almost out of sight. If someone had had a feather handy, Mrs. Potts and Mrs. Ray could have been knocked over right there in the street with no trouble at all.

"My land!" exclaimed Mrs. Potts, jerking back to life, "Look what the wind blew in!"

Her companion emitted a long hiss of breath. Her gaze struck the man's retreating back so forcefully, it's a wonder he didn't feel hot darts between his shoulder blades.

"If my memory serves, Mrs. Potts, it's an ill wind that blows no good," Mrs. Ray returned with a kind of perverse satisfaction. Mrs. Ray was a stern, bony, narrow-eyed woman who wallowed in pessimism. Already she saw storm clouds descending upon the neighborhood.

Mrs. Potts twitched her bonnet in agreement. She never forgot a single misdeed in the village.

"You're right, Mrs. Ray. Remember that awful ruckus last time he was in Avonlea?"

"And at the funeral, of all places. Well, I suppose nothing's sacred to some people."

Both women drew together disapprovingly, but their eyes gleamed in anticipation of some renewed upheaval in Avonlea. The object of their interest, quite far down the road now, strode along vigorously. Despite his citified dress, he seemed to know exactly where he was going. As he went, he gazed about him at the wintry landscape, his step increasingly buoyant, until he was well out of sight.

Not far down that same road lay the King farm, its prosperous acres spreading around a big, friendly farmhouse and a weathered, gray barn set firmly on a high, fieldstone foundation. Inside the barn, at that very moment, Alec King was leading the way across the barn floor towards a hulking shape that sat in the gloom, all covered with dust and bits of straw. Two of his three children, Felicity and Felix, followed at his heels, in company with their cousin, Sara Stanley. Alec was grinning very much like a man with a surprise up his sleeve. His grin was shared by Felix and Felicity. Alex paused dramatically, grabbed the corner of the shape, and suddenly whipped the cover off a wonderful, old-fashioned, two-horse sleigh. The sleigh was painted bright red, with long, slender runners curved high in front, and seats enough for the whole King family.

"There's the old cutter. What do you think?"

The drama had all been for Sara's benefit, for Sara had lived most of her life in Montreal and never seen a real country sleigh.

She let out a delighted squeal. "It's beautiful, Uncle Alec."

Alec chuckled. Sara could always be counted on for a gratifying reaction. He knew the sleigh would delight this irrepressible twelve-year-old who had so unexpectedly come to live with her Avonlea relatives in the last year. Though Sara's warm, often headlong enthusiasm for life got her into trouble again and again, it was that very same quality that soon won hearts and made everyone want to please her. Walking around the front of the cutter, Alec patted the elegantly arching dash.

"Yes, indeed, and we haven't had her out since last year's skating party."

The Avonlea skating party was the jolliest of all Avonlea social events. Sara, who had been hearing of nothing else from her cousins for weeks, had her heart set on whirling and gliding merrily over the frozen pond. Since her father had sent her away from Montreal some months before, Sara had had to adjust to a great many things about life in the country. Some—like the strict ideas of her Aunt Hetty, with whom she lived—had come as a shock. Some—like Avonlea parties and running about with her King cousins—had proved quite wonderful. Sara had got through spring, summer and fall. Now, with the ground frozen hard and the air tingling with hints of snow, Sara looked forward to sampling all the delights winter in Avonlea had to offer.

"Here, Sara, try this."

Felicity, who was almost fourteen, reached into the cutter and pulled out a heavy bearskin rug used to keep the the sleigh riders wrapped up snug and warm against the biting winter winds. Sara pressed the rough brown fur against her cheek, already imagining the jingle of sleigh bells and the hiss of runners over the pristine white road. Passionately, she hoped drifts and drifts of snow would fall so that the big cutter could come out of storage and carry them all, laughing and shouting, to the skating party.

"Oh, I love fur rugs. They're always so warm and cozy."

Besides being Felicity's cousin, Sara was also her best friend, though this state of affairs hadn't come about easily. Felicity hadn't taken well to the intrusion of a city-bred cousin with a trunkful of Paris dresses and a nanny of her own. Aunt Hetty, eldest of the King clan and also the Avonlea schoolmistress, had got rid of the nanny pretty quickly and taken Sara firmly in hand.

However, Sara had turned out to have more imagination than the Kings had ever encountered before, and a talent for getting herself calamitously mixed up in other people's affairs. Felicity had all but lost count of the scrapes Sara's farfetched ideas had led them all into. Yet, since Sara's heart had always been in the right place, it was hard not to fall under her charm. Now Felicity couldn't imagine what she'd do without Sara around to make life interesting.

Felix, eleven, liked Sara too. Just the thought of having her at the skating party threw him into a festive mood. Dashing suddenly behind the sleigh, he scooped up an armful of hay and tossed it playfully at his father.

"Yahoo!" he cried, as the hay caught his father on the side of the shoulder.

Alex batted it aside with a laugh and ducked his head in mock-menace.

"All right, Felix King, you're in trouble now!"

Turning boyish himself, Alec ran after his son, caught him by the tail of his coat and tossed him into a heap of straw. Instantly, Felicity and Sara jumped into the game, throwing more hay all over Alec. This rough-and-tumble family life was something Sara had never known in her sheltered existence before Avonlea, and she plunged into it with delight. Before Alec knew it, the three children had ganged up on him, flinging great handfuls of hay and tangling his legs so that he, too, went rolling onto the barn floor along with Felix. Shrieking with delight, the children bolted for the door as Alec scrambled to his feet again and made lumbering attempts to catch them.

"I'm going to get you for that," he growled, giving them a head start and then thumping after them into the open barnyard.

Screaming and giggling, the three children flung themselves out of the barn, making a fumbling attempt to close the door behind them. They were too late. Alec was already pushing through it and making grabs in their direction.

Felix and Sara might have made a clean getaway, but Felicity, in front of them, tripped, and all three went tumbling down into a squealing tangle.

Sara, her tam all askew, was just squirming out from under Felix's feet when she caught sight of a tall, masculine figure leaning against the fence, watching all the exuberant horseplay—the very same man who had alighted from the coach in Avonlea. As though struck by an unseen thunderbolt, Sara went utterly still, her eyes as big as silver coins.

"Papa!" she whispered, completely heedless of Felicity and Felix tumbling sideways against her and getting clumsily to their knees.

They no sooner had their balance than Sara knocked them to the ground again as she exploded upright and began to race toward the man.

"Papa," she cried now, at the top of her lungs, her face transformed with joy. "Papa!"

"Sara!"

Blair Stanley dropped his valise to the ground and was already swinging one long leg over the barnyard fence in total disregard of his expensive tailoring. His rugged face was lit up just as much as Sara's.

Luckily, he got both legs over the fence in time to take the impact of the flying girl as she launched herself bodily against him. In a single, fluid motion, he lifted her effortlessly into the air and swung her round and round.

"I've missed you so much," Sara choked out.

"Oh, I missed you too."

"I was so afraid..."

The rest of the words were cut off as Sara was swung round again and then gathered into her father's strong arms.

"I'm glad to see you." The visitor spoke quickly, his voice rough with emotion, his whole manner saying that the things Sara was afraid about didn't have to be spoken of any more.

Felix and Felicity were so astonished by Sara's behavior that they remained on their knees, staring up at this striking stranger. Their father came to a halt beside them, almost as taken aback.

"Look who that is!" he whistled, hauling Felicity to her feet and scrambling to regain his own composure. "That's Blair—Sara's father. Well, well."

Chapter Two

Over in the King farmhouse, no one had any inkling of their startling new visitor. Andrew King was bringing in an armload of wood and dumping it in the woodbox to keep the big, wood-burning stove in fuel. In winter, the kitchen stove was the cozy heart of any farmhouse. People pulled their chairs next to it, dried their wet mitts over it, toasted their cold toes on the oven door and dipped hot water from its capacious reservoir.

And, of course, they cooked on it, which was just what Janet King, Alec's wife, was doing at that moment. She stirred a pot of stew and kept her eye on the vegetables. Her youngest child, Cecily, ten, set the table for the midday meal.

"Oh, thank you, Andrew." Janet smiled as the wood tumbled from the boy's arms.

Andrew, about Felicity's age, was another King cousin seeking refuge in Avonlea. His father, Alan, Alec's brother, was a geologist working in South America. While he was gone, Andrew stayed with his uncle and aunt and enjoyed a happy home life. It seemed the Kings of Avonlea had room enough and hearts big enough to take in any waif or stray among them who needed shelter.

This peaceful scene was shattered as Felix and Felicity burst in through the door, their faces glowing from cold air and galloping excitement.

"Mother, Mother," Felix panted, almost getting jammed in the doorway in his efforts to beat his sister inside.

"Uncle Blair's here!" Felicity cut in, triumphantly taking advantage of Felix's loss of breath to break the momentous news. Wealthy, cosmopolitan Blair Stanley was a figure of mythic proportions in the children's minds, and Felicity could still scarcely believe he was here in flesh and blood.

"*I* wanted to tell her, Felicity," Felix protested, feeling cheated of a tremendous scoop. Felix didn't often get one up on his sister though he felt honor-bound to keep on trying.

Teasingly, Felicity stuck her tongue out at Felix just as her mother dropped the spoon she was using to stir the stew.

"Uncle Blair?" Janet croaked, not even noticing the spoon sink out of sight in the bubbling pot.

"Yes."

Felix stuck his tongue back out at Felicity and hopped from one foot to the other, relishing this unexpected break in farm routine. Both children still had their outdoor boots on—a major sin in the King kitchen—but their mother didn't notice. In fact, Janet was quite dumfounded, as if she hadn't been able to credit her own ears.

"Wha...you...Blair...is here?"

The last time Blair had been in Avonlea had been nine years before when he had come to bury his wife, formerly Ruth King, in the Avonlea family plot. Ruth had died, tragically young, of tuberculosis, leaving her husband and three-year-old Sara behind. Hetty had openly accused Blair of bringing on Ruth's death. Blair had sworn never to set foot in Avonlea again. The uproar hadn't died down for months. And now here was Blair in the King farmhouse, just a hop and a skip away from Rose Cottage where Hetty lived. Janet cringed to think what might happen with those two firebrands within striking distance of each other.

"Yes!" cried Felix again, completely unaware of old family quarrels and delighted that he had managed to throw his mother into such confusion.

"Oh, no...oh, good gracious. Oh well, isn't that just like Blair Stanley—no letter, no telegram."

Frantically, Janet began to pat at her hair and tug at the apron she had on, her oldest one—as luck would have it, with fruit stains all down the front from a summer of making jam. She'd barely yanked the apron off when she heard the outside door opening again.

"Janet?" floated Alec's voice. "You'll never believe who's here."

Alec and Blair came tramping into the front hall with a radiant Sara, still clinging to her father's side. Janet scurried in to greet him, with Felicity, Felix and Cecily running energetically behind.

"Oh, well! Blair Stanley, this is a surprise."

Just how much of a surprise she didn't dare say. She still hadn't caught her breath and was trying hard to get a grip on herself.

"Isn't it wonderful, Aunt Janet?" Sara chirped ecstatically. She hadn't seen her father since she had left Montreal. His arrival in Avonlea was the most wonderful event she could imagine.

Even if he hadn't been Sara's father, Blair was still a man who made his presence felt in any room he stepped into. His cashmere scarf and fine wool topcoat contrasted vividly with the homey, rural furnishings of the farmhouse. Now he stopped in the middle of pulling off kid gloves to beam delightedly down at Janet, taking in the brood behind her.

"Janet, it's good to see you. And look how this family's grown."

Flustered, Janet turned sideways so that her children could all be seen. She was very proud of them and took immediate refuge in motherly fondness.

"Oh, yes, Cecily and Felix weren't even in this world yet..." She paused, putting her hand to her forehead. "Oh no, I'm wrong. Felix was only two years old when Ruth..."

When agitated, tact was not Janet King's strong point. The last word was no sooner out than she screeched to a halt in the midst of an

embarrassed silence. An undefined emotion flicker-
ed across Blair's face, and Sara swallowed.

"Here," Alec said, jumping in quickly, "let me
take your coat."

Alec was already holding Sara's coat but put it
down in order to take that of his brother-in-law.
Sara, who couldn't be close enough to her father,
reached up for it instead.

"I'll take it, Papa."

While Sara was busily hanging the garment on
the coatrack, Alec leaned, with a wink, towards
Blair.

"You must have some good news for us, man.
Tell us about the trial."

The reason Sara had been sent to live with her
practically unknown King relatives had been
because her father wanted her far out of range of
scandal. And Prince Edward Island was about as
far as one could get. Blair Stanley's business partner had been dishonest, and Blair had been
blamed too. It had been a long, weary wait of
many months for the case to come to trial. And
now here was Blair, large as life, in Avonlea, and
obviously not in jail.

"There's not much to tell," Blair drawled with
the mock-casualness of a man wanting to draw
out the suspense.

Alec and Janet couldn't stand much suspense. Janet tugged at her cuffs, failing to notice that Blair's eyes were dancing.

"Oh, now, Blair, we've all been watching the papers..."

Blair burst into a gleaming smile and slapped his thigh in triumph.

"I have been acquitted on the embezzlement charges!"

Acquitted! Gladness flooded the King household. The business about the charges and trial had been a cloud over all the Kings ever since the trouble was known. Though the family generally didn't speak about it, Sara had suffered, even in Avonlea. Blair Stanley's trouble had been reported in the newspapers and had become common knowledge. Some of Sara's nastier schoolmates had tried taunting her about it, though it was a mistake they didn't make again once they encountered Sara's spirited retaliation.

"Good for you!" Alec rumbled, congratulating Blair with a solid pat on the back.

Sara, quite beside herself, almost dropped her father's coat on the floor when she heard. She bounded back from the coatrack to hug her father again.

"Papa, that's wonderful."

Never again would she have to endure those

awful jibes, or lie awake at night worrying that policemen would take her father away and put him behind bars. Blair picked her up and gave her a little swing again.

"Yes, so, with all that behind us," he announced, "we can get back to our life. I can now take Sara home."

Blair might as well have tossed a bomb into the hall and watched it go off. There was a prolonged moment of dumfounded silence. Then everyone's face fell, including Sara's.

"Home?" repeated Felicity in a small voice. She and Sara had already made plans for the whole winter, including what they were going to recite together at the Christmas pageant and what they were going to do for Aunt Olivia's birthday. Sara couldn't go away now!

Alec frowned at this new development. Events were moving far too fast for his taste.

"When do you, uh, plan on leaving, Blair?"

"I've booked return tickets...for tomorrow."

Blair smiled down expecting Sara to be pleased. All Sara could do was gasp. "Tomorrow? Papa..."

"But you can't leave that soon," Felicity protested before Sara could even get out the rest of her plea. Why, it was almost as though Sara were being kidnapped from under Felicity's nose.

"You'll miss the skating party," Cecily piped up—an enormous tragedy in her young eyes. She'd been looking forward so much to showing Sara how to roast chestnuts in the big bonfire that kept everyone warm at the pond.

Afraid she'd soon have wails of complaint from all concerned, Janet King clapped her hands.

"All right, now, that's enough. Let's go. Set the table. Off you go. You too, Sara. Come on, your father must be famished."

Janet shooed the children into the kitchen. As she followed them, she gave Alec a swift prod in the ribs. "Do something," she whispered urgently. Goodness knows what would result if Blair actually carried out his plan.

Alec turned back to his brother-in-law, deciding to try bluff good humor and hospitality.

"You shouldn't be in such a rush about leaving, Blair. We, uh, country folk don't take well to sudden change. You know that."

Blair only looked sober and tucked his thumbs into his waistcoat.

"Alec, I appreciate everything that's been done for Sara during my, uh, difficulty. But you know what I'm up against with Hetty. I think it's best that I leave right away."

Alec was afraid he knew only too well what Blair was up against, though he certainly wasn't going to speculate out loud at the moment. Hetty had very strong views about family loyalty. She had never forgiven Blair for wooing Ruth away from Avonlea, showering her with gifts and whisking her off to all sorts of outlandish places, like England and Italy, where no sane person had any business going. Now there was no way Hetty could be expected to relinquish Sara without a strenuous fight.

As Blair went into the kitchen, where so many wonderful smells promised a country feast, Janet popped past him for a moment alone with her husband.

"Alec, shouldn't someone go over and tell Olivia and Hetty?"

Even Alec's courage failed at the thought of undertaking that dangerous mission. The windows would probably shake when Hetty discovered Blair Stanley in the neighborhood.

"Maybe we should wait," he advised hastily. "We can at least have our dinner in peace."

Janet opened her mouth to insist, then closed it again at Alec's stubborn expression. All the Kings were stubborn. And Alec, though he was the most easygoing of the lot, could dig his heels in as much as the others. Sighing, Janet hurried back to the stove to put the kettle on and retrieve the spoon from the stew.

Chapter Three

Rose Cottage, just over the hill from the King farmhouse, was a charming place with a wide veranda and pretty scrollwork ornamenting its gables. Though all unsuspecting of the larger upheaval about to befall it, Rose Cottage was not without smaller commotions of its own. At just about the same moment Blair Stanley was arriving at the King farm, a buggy was pulling up to the cottage door.

The appearance of the buggy had a rather immediate effect upon Hetty King, who, until that moment, had been dusting and humming and feeling quite content with life. She dropped the duster abruptly onto the parlor side table, let out a sharp, disapproving breath and stood glaring through the curtains at the lanky figure descending from the buggy's seat.

The lanky figure belonged to Jasper Dale, known locally as the Awkward Man. Jasper came by the name honestly. His gangling limbs tripped over things, dropped things and got themselves into a knot whenever possible. What put them into knots was the proximity of other people. Until Sara and her Aunt Olivia had taken him in hand, Jasper had lived like a recluse on the edge of Avonlea, tinkering in his workshop, avoiding human beings and generally acting like the shiest man alive.

Olivia had changed all that when she discovered that Jasper not only had a camera but a darkroom, too, and could take the loveliest photographs when he wanted to. As it happened, Olivia had been offered a job writing up local events for the Avonlea *Chronicle*—providing she could come up with pictures to match. Olivia hadn't rested until she persuaded Jasper Dale out of his solitude to accompany her on her reporting trips as her photographer. The fact that Olivia was a charming young woman who seemed to enjoy his company had a lot to do with Jasper's capitulation. One got a feeling that there wasn't a great deal Jasper Dale wouldn't do for Olivia King, from walking over red-hot coals to braving the main street of Avonlea just to walk by her side.

Yet, though Jasper might walk over hot coals for Olivia, an approach to Rose Cottage's front door was almost beyond his capacity. Behind that front door was Hetty King. Hetty thought Jasper a poor specimen of manhood indeed, and had no patience at all for his bumbling, clumsy ways.

Knowing Hetty's opinion of him very well, Jasper stood by the buggy wheel, shifting from one foot to the other, trying to screw up his courage. For no reason at all, he took a blanket out of his buggy. Then he put it back. Next, he crammed his hat onto his head, only to snatch it away again, remembering that gentlemen always approached a lady's door bareheaded, especially if that lady happened to be Hetty King. Finally, hat in hand, Jasper swallowed hard and sidled up to the door, as though expecting it to fly open upon a brimstone-breathing dragon. He knocked timidly, turned away, inspected his hat brim and almost looked as though he might make a run for it after all, when Hetty flung open the door.

"Yes?" she inquired, so forbiddingly that poor Jasper almost bolted on the spot. When he was unnerved, his stutter almost strangled him. His terrible stutter was one of the chief reasons Jasper avoided everyone in Avonlea.

"Um, Miss K-K-K-K—"

"King?" Hetty finished for him glacially. She was a tall, thin woman with hair drawn back severely into a bun. Her many years of teaching school made her an expert at freezing people where they stood.

"King." Jasper gulped and bravely took another run at communicating. "Um, I've come to call for Miss K-K-K...uh, Olivia," he finished shakily, lest Hetty, by some wild mischance, assume it was her he had come to collect.

"Oh...is that so?"

Hetty looked Jasper up and down, frowning at his free use of her younger sister's first name. Then she stepped back into the house. When Jasper, foolishly thinking this a gesture of hospitality, made to follow, Hetty slammed the door an inch from his astonished nose.

"Olivia!" Hetty bellowed once inside, her single, grudging concession to Jasper Dale's presence.

Instantly, Olivia herself came dashing down the stairs into the front hall of Rose Cottage. Very much in a rush, she sped right past Hetty and into the kitchen, looking about her distractedly.

"Oh, my goodness, I don't know where I've left my little black notebook."

Hetty showed no interest in the notebook. Instead, she fixed her sister with a gimlet eye. She saw that Olivia had on her favorite gray wool suit and her blouse with the real lace on the collar. Most incriminating was the jet brooch that had belonged to Grandmother King, pinned at Olivia's throat. Olivia only took it out of its box on what she felt were special occasions.

"You didn't say anything to me about going to that lecture with Jasper Dale."

Hetty liked everything around her to run with smooth predictability. She hated any break in her careful order. Before the *Chronicle* had offered Olivia this job, Olivia had been content to stay home and keep house while Hetty taught. Now Olivia's head seemed quite turned with all the gadding about she had to do to get her stories. Things at Rose Cottage were getting more and more unsettled every day.

"Jasper's only accompanying me to take a photograph. That's all, Hetty," Olivia tossed back airily, still searching for the notebook.

Olivia was proud of her new job and proud of having coaxed Avonlea's most reclusive bachelor out of his darkroom and into the light of day. She didn't seem to mind, as Hetty minded very much, that Jasper Dale was still awkward and tongue-tied. The Kings had a position to maintain in the community, Hetty felt. To her mind, Jasper was not at all suitable to escort someone as refined as Olivia King.

"Humph! Gallivanting all over the Island with that—"

"Oh, I would hardly call going to the town

hall in Markdale 'gallivanting,'" Olivia cut in, with more spirit than she was wont to show with her dominating older sister. Something about Jasper brought out all Olivia's protective instincts.

Pouncing on the notebook, Olivia pattered back to the hall and began pinning on a blue felt hat with a rather startlingly jaunty bunch of feathers on the side.

"How do you like my new hat?" Olivia asked, tilting the brim perkily in the mirror. "I bought it with my first paycheck from the *Chronicle*."

Practical Hetty sniffed at such frivolous use of hard-earned money. Besides, she was fighting back the awful suspicion that the new hat had something to do with Jasper Dale.

"I don't really think blue is your color, Olivia," she commented repressively, growing a little desperate now to stem this outbreak of foolishness in her youngest sister. Olivia had always been sweet-natured and pliant, giving in to Hetty's more mature wisdom. Now, this new-found independence was upsetting the organized life she valued so much and had worked so hard to establish at Rose Cottage.

Her comment had absolutely no effect on

Olivia, who now flew to the door, eyes already sparkling with anticipation of the afternoon.

"Well...don't wait supper for me," she called back over her shoulder. "Oh, and Sara asked me to tell you that she'll be having dinner with the children at Janet's."

Hetty's lips drew into a thin, tight line, covering her twitch of disappointment. Though she would never admit it out loud, she always looked forward to Sara's animated chatter at the dinner table.

"I spend so much time on my own these days, I might as well be living on my own, not that anyone cares..."

"Goodbye, Hetty," Olivia sang out without stopping to listen. In a wink, she had flitted out and slammed the door behind her.

"...about me," Hetty finished, the echo of the door ringing in her ears.

Hetty went to the window and saw Jasper helping Olivia up into his buggy. They were both laughing merrily. Jasper seemed to have found it in himself to answer Olivia quite volubly, despite being practically speechless only minutes before at the door. In fact, now that Hetty looked closely, she noticed that Jasper had produced, from his long-neglected wardrobe, something approximating a respectable suit.

Of course, Hetty would never have gone so far as to admit that Jasper could, when he stopped ducking and bobbing, cut a fine, manly figure as he gathered up the reins and turned the buggy around. Hetty only saw her younger sister leaving her without a backward glance—to go off with a man. She and Olivia had lived together in Rose Cottage so long, their life seemed so settled, that the idea of Olivia taking an interest in some-one, even Jasper Dale, filled Hetty with a queer feeling very like panic. Hetty regarded herself as more of a mother than a sister to Olivia, and with the addition of Sara Stanley to the household, the little family felt quite complete.

Hetty turned away from the scene outside and went in search of her duster. Surely Olivia wouldn't let Jasper Dale and all this nonsense about a job turn her head. And if Olivia was going to gad about the country chasing newspaper stories, thank goodness there was still Sara, who could always be relied upon to keep Hetty company, and make Rose Cottage seem like a home.

Chapter Four

Hetty would have been in a much worse state had she known what was going on just down the lane at the King farmhouse. Though Sara had been too excited to eat much, the rest of the Kings had put away a hearty dinner, all of them talking at once to their debonair guest. Afterwards, they pushed their chairs comfortably back from the table, still exchanging news while Sara and Felicity cleared away the plates. Even as she walked around with an armful of china, Sara couldn't get enough of her father.

"Blair, this is such a pleasant surprise," Janet was saying warmly. She had managed to get over most of her astonishment at Blair's sudden appearance and was now exerting herself to make him welcome. Perhaps she was also trying to keep him in the kitchen as long as she could to delay the inevitable confrontation with Hetty.

Meanwhile, Felicity was trying to organize her own delaying tactics. While the grown-ups were absorbed in their own talk, Felicity dragged Sara off into a corner of the kitchen.

"Sara, you can't possibly go so soon," she whispered urgently.

Sara carefully set down a stack of dessert

plates, the good ones, which Janet had hastily extracted from the china cabinet in Blair's honor. Luckily, there had been one of Felicity's plump, brown apple pies for dessert. Felicity prided herself on her baking.

"What else can I do?" Sara asked anxiously, still reeling from the events of the last hour or so.

Felicity's gaze darted significantly at Blair Stanley.

"Talk to him."

If there was anything Sara could do well, it was talk. The number of adventures the King children had got involved in on her account were testimony themselves to Sara's powers of persuasion.

As Sara approached her father on this mission, Janet laughed aloud. Blair had been telling them all about his trip from Montreal to Prince Edward Island—a complicated process that involved several changes of trains and a long ride on the ferry over to the island province.

"Alec, remember the last time we took the ferry?" Janet said nostalgically. With the children and the farm to look after, they hadn't been able to travel for ages.

Alec grinned at the recollection.

"I tell you, it was so rough the fish got seasick."

Everybody had a fine chuckle. Then Blair, replete with a good meal and good fellowship, straightened and turned to his daughter.

"Well, Sara, my dear, we should pick up your things at Rose Cottage, because I've booked rooms for us at the hotel in Markdale."

This information quite wiped out the speech Sara had been composing in her head. A hotel was so contrary to King hospitality that Sara's mouth dropped open.

"Hotel? Papa, I don't want to stay in a hotel. Stay with me at Rose Cottage."

Alec and Janet exchanged nervous glances. Blair Stanley hastily cleared his throat.

"Sara, I have it on good authority from Nanny Louisa that there is a great lack of accommodation there."

And Nanny Louisa's views were bound to be biased, since it was from Rose Cottage that Hetty had sent her almost instantly packing, declaring it simply scandalous that a twelve-year-old girl should have her own nursemaid and not learn to look after herself.

"Blair, you're more than welcome to stay with us," Alec broke in, trying to head off the trouble before it had time to brew.

"Please, Papa?" Sara pleaded. She had a hundred things to show her father around Avonlea and simply couldn't bear it if they went off to the Markdale hotel.

Blair hesitated. As a businessman, hotels were a normal procedure with him. However, he was enjoying himself enormously with Alec and Janet, who seemed genuinely to want him to stay in their house.

"I don't want to impose."

Blair had a strong independent streak, and wanted to be under obligation to no one. Seeing this, Alec gave him a comradely thump on the shoulder.

"You're not imposing, man. You're family!" Sara's pleading eyes ensured Blair's surrender.

"All right. Thank you." He stood up and shoved back his chair. "Sara, it's going to be a long day tomorrow, so you get your coat and I'll walk you home."

Janet King shot Alec another frantic look, but Alec had done all he could for the time being. The two could only watch helplessly as Sara, trying to smile at the others, went obediently to pull on her overcoat. The moment of truth could be put off no longer.

Blair followed Sara outside and, in a very short time, the two of them were walking hand in hand over the well-worn lane between the

King farmhouse and nearby Rose Cottage. It was a lane Sara and her cousins had scampered over dozens of times on their way back and forth to visit each other. The noisy, roomy King household was as much a home to Sara as Rose Cottage. After growing up in pampered solitude in Montreal, the discovery of this big, extended family in Avonlea had been one of the great joys of her life. Now, even though Sara was very happy to have her father beside her, she was terribly torn over the way he planned to whisk her so suddenly away from the life she had come to love so fervently.

"Papa, I do want to stay for the Avonlea skating party," she told him earnestly. "All my friends will be there, and I want to prove to them I have a father. I think I just want to stay here for a little while longer. I'm not ready to leave yet."

To Sara, this request seemed a very reasonable compromise. She wanted very much to be with her father, yet being with her father meant being without Avonlea. She had so many mixed up feeling whirling around inside her, she had no idea how she'd ever get them sorted out.

Seeing they were almost at their destination, Blair bent his head towards his daughter's, his breath making little clouds in the crisp, late-afternoon air. The frozen pebbles crunched under their feet and a brown winter sparrow lit on the old rail fence nearby as if to hear the answer.

"Sara, I know how you must feel, but it's imperative that I get back—"

The rest was broken off by the sight of a buggy just rolling to a halt in front of Rose Cottage. Sara hopped with delight and tugged her father forward.

"Look, there's Aunt Olivia! Come and say hello."

"Olivia..." Blair said the name almost to himself, as if evoking memories from a time long before Sara could remember.

Sara was now literally dragging her father over to where Jasper Dale was helping Olivia from her seat. From the giggles and the flushed cheeks, Jasper and Olivia had obviously had a fine time together at the lecture.

"Aunt Olivia," Sara shouted, "my Papa's here."

Olivia was so surprised she would have fallen the rest of the way out of the buggy if Jasper hadn't caught her. She hastily righted herself and stared at the handsome man approaching.

"Blair Stanley! Whatever are you doing here?"

Blair didn't answer that question. Instead, his face lit up with genuine warmth at the sight of the youngest King sister.

"Olivia, you have turned into quite a beauty," Blair exclaimed, with all the charm and gallantry he could use so well. He remembered Olivia as a long-legged girl being rather forcefully brought up by Hetty.

Olivia blushed and waved her glove towards the buggy.

"Oh, Blair, um, I'd like you to meet Jasper Dale. Jasper Dale, Blair Stanley."

Meeting strangers was not Jasper's forte—especially confident, well-dressed strangers who strewed compliments at Olivia's feet. Jasper thought Olivia a beauty too, but would sooner have been hung by his thumbs for a week than try to get up the courage to say so.

"Ummm..." he mumbled, taking a death-grip on his hat.

"Good to meet you, Mr. Dale," Blair returned genially, extending his hand.

Jasper nodded at the hand and backed into the buggy wheel. The buggy rocked on its springs and the horse tossed its head in alarm.

"Well, um, it's a...Miss King, I'd be better suited to, ah, you know, be on my way."

Before Olivia could stop him, Jasper had

heaved himself up onto the buggy seat and grasped the reins.

"Nice to have, um, nice to have met you. Goodbye."

"Mr. Dale! Wait," Sara cried. Jasper Dale was one of her own special friends, and she wanted her father to get to know him.

She was too late. Jasper was already making his getaway. The biggest concession Sara got was a final wave, just before Jasper and the buggy vanished in a cloud of dust down the road.

Olivia let out a sigh, at once tolerant and exasperated. She knew very well that, unless physically held in place, Jasper would flee in the face of a man like Blair Stanley, but she wished Jasper would stay, at least until Blair saw through the awkwardness to the cleverness and ingenuity inside. The more Olivia saw of Jasper, the more she began to think of him, in his own peculiar way, as one of the most interesting fellows in Avonlea.

"Jasper works with me. He takes wonderful photographs," she supplied enthusiastically in an effort to make up for Jasper's defection.

"Oh, yes," smiled Blair. "Sara wrote and told me about your job with the newspaper."

Realizing they were all standing outside in a

cold, blustery breeze, Olivia suddenly remembered herself as hostess.

"Now, Blair, you must come in. I won't hear of
you being in Avonlea without coming in to pay
your respects to Rose Cottage."

Blair remained standing where he was, his
face sobering. He really intended just walking
Sara as far as the door.

"Olivia, I really shouldn't."

"Oh, of course you can, Papa," Sara burst out.
"You can stay here as long as you want."

Sara would have realized how reckless that
promise was had she seen her Aunt Hetty. Hetty
had been upstairs straightening things in Sara's
room. Tidying Sara's room was one of the ways
Hetty could fuss over the child without being
caught in the act. Hetty had just been fluffing a
cushion on Sara's little armchair when she
glanced out the window and caught sight of Blair
Stanley.

She froze on the spot. Indeed, Blair Stanley's
appearance seemed to have the same effect on
Hetty as a specter rising up from the midnight
gloom. Suddenly short of breath, she twitched the
curtain open a crack and stepped back so that she
could see. Blair glanced up just in time to catch
the curtain swinging. However, there was no way
he could refuse Olivia's invitation. With a rather

grim, fatalistic look, he followed Olivia and Sara to the front door.

Chapter Five

Once inside Rose Cottage, Sara tossed her coat onto the chair in the hall and ran into the parlor, expecting her father to be at her heels. Slowly, Blair closed the front door behind him. Olivia took his things and then, still flustered, said she was going into the kitchen that very minute to make them all a nice cup of tea. After Olivia had gone, Blair paused, glanced warily up the stairs, then followed Sara into the parlor, the place where every important guest was entertained.

Sara had dreamed often of being reunited with her father. Now that she had him on her home ground, she naturally wanted to show him everything. She even went so far as to open the darkly gleaming piano in the corner and pick out a tune.

"This is mama's piano. Do you remember it, Papa?"

Even to be allowed to touch the piano had been the occasion of a struggle with Hetty. Ruth King had been the musical one of the family, filling Rose

Cottage with lilting piano melodies and bursts of song. After Ruth was gone, Hetty had kept the instrument in the parlor, closed and silent, as a monument to her departed sister. Yet even Hetty was forced to admit that a piano wasn't much good if nobody played it. Eventually, the combined efforts of Sara and Olivia had broken Hetty down.

Blair Stanley's face took on a soft, faraway look, as though he remembered the piano very well.

"Yes," he murmured. "In fact, I think she used to play that same piece."

"I know," returned Sara wistfully. "Aunt Olivia told me that this was her music book. Look at this."

She held out a well-thumbed collection with roses elaborately embossed on its cover. Opening the front, Sara pointed out an inscription written in bold, flowing script. It said, "To Ruth—All my love, Blair." Blair's face changed yet again, as though actually seeing Ruth King with the music book open in front of her.

"I gave that book to your mother on her twenty-first birthday."

Walking over, he picked up the picture of Ruth that stood atop the piano and gazed at the slender young woman in it. Then he smiled at his daughter. Ruth had been high-spirited and full of artistic fancies and there was so much of her in Sara.

While Blair and Sara hovered about the piano, indulging in memories, Hetty had been thrown into utter consternation about what she should do. First she stood rigidly in Sara's room, clutching the cushion she had been smoothing. Then she dropped the cushion and crushed her handkerchief. Finally, she tiptoed down the stairs and into the front hall, furtively hugging the wall so she couldn't be seen from the parlor. Brows knotted fiercely, she darted past and into the kitchen.

Hetty entered to find Olivia doing her hurried best to get together some refreshments for their guest. Olivia was still so unsettled by Blair's arrival that she banged the tea service against the table and came within a hair of dropping the good china teapot with the violets on it. Taking a deep breath, she steadied the cups with shaking hands. All the worse for her nerves, Hetty marched up behind her and whispered violently into her ear.

"Olivia—"

Olivia jumped three inches and nearly lost the whole tea service onto the floor.

"Oh! Oh! Hetty, you startled me!"

Finally managing to slide the tea tray to safety, Olivia ran one hand across her forehead and began to reach for the ginger cookies, which were kept in a jar on the kitchen sideboard. Hetty blocked her path.

"I want that man out. I need time to think what we're to do!"

Chin quivering, eyes ablaze, Hetty was rapidly working herself up for a full-scale war.

"To do about what?" Olivia asked in wonder, trying to keep hold of the cookie jar and stare at her sister at the same time.

"About Sara, of course. Oh, really, Olivia, sometimes I wonder what's there between your ears."

"Hetty, I don't understand..."

"Shhhh!" Hetty sputtered, with a glance towards the parlor. "Believe me, I will not let go of Sara as easily as I did our Ruth."

"Let go? Hetty, calm down! He's not taking her—"

Scornfully, Hetty let out a hiss of breath.

"Don't be naive, Olivia. Blair knows he's not welcome. Yet he's here. Oh, he'll spirit that child away all right, before we can blink an eye."

"I believe you're mistaken." Unable to imagine such a thing, Olivia rapidly began piling ginger cookies onto a plate. Sara was part of Rose

Cottage now. Why would anybody want to take her away?

Hetty grimaced in frustration.

"Olivia..."

Oblivious to the battle raging in the kitchen, Blair and Sara sat together on the big horsehair sofa in the parlor, also rather warmly discussing the immediate future. Sara had tackled her father again about leaving so soon and he was showing no sign whatever of yielding to her arguments.

"I know, Sara," Blair was saying patiently, "but I've already explained..."

Olivia walked in carrying the hastily laden tea tray. The tea service rattled precariously, and a pyramid of cookies threatened to spill over the side.

"Well, here we go," announced Olivia, as heartily as she could after the scene in the kitchen. Sweet and pliant by nature, Olivia felt more shaken up than the teacups by the confrontation with her sister.

"Where's Aunt Hetty?" Sara asked, peering over Olivia's shoulder.

Telltale spots of color leaped into Olivia's cheeks. The tea sloshed inside the pot and the cups jiggled in their saucers before Olivia managed to get the tray down on the side table. One

more second and her fluttery hands would have
betrayed her altogether.

"Hetty is, uh, I called up to her and she's, um..."

Olivia was hopeless at lying, and Blair knew
very well what her confusion meant. His face
darkened.

"Huh—I think it would be better if I were on
my way."

Abandoned by Olivia in the kitchen, Hetty
had tiptoed surreptitiously out into the front hall
again, where she could hear the conversation.
Stealth didn't suit Hetty one bit. She jammed herself halfway behind the coatrack; her head stuck
out, her elbows stuck out, and her mouth grew so
tight her lips almost disappeared from her face.
She heard Blair rising to his feet.

"If Hetty wanted to see me, she'd be down
here by now," Blair said stiffly.

"Please don't leave yet, Papa," Sara begged,
seeing the pleasant visit about to collapse in failure.

Blair patted her soothingly.

"Now, young lady, you get a good night's
sleep, 'cause we've got a big day tomorrow, and
you've got to be packed and ready first thing in
the morning."

Now Olivia's mouth dropped open. Unbe-
lievably, Hetty had been right!

"First thing? Oh, Blair, no," she protested.

"You'll stay here at Rose Cottage for a few days, at least. I'm sure Hetty will agree once I've spoken with her."

Agree! Hetty's bosom heaved furiously. Gathering up her skirts, she swept into the parlor looking so outraged that Olivia jumped back and Sara gaped.

"Why, Blair Stanley," Hetty blazed. "Well, you're the last person I expected to see standing in my parlor this frosty winter afternoon."

Hetty's incensed state of mind was clear for all to see. Blair, taken off guard as he was, made a heroic effort to rise to the occasion.

"Hetty, what a pleasure it is to see you again," he said civilly. "I want you to know how much I appreciate what you've done for Sara. I need only look at her to see how well she's been taken care of."

"There's no need to flatter me," Hetty snapped.

Blair still hung on to his manners.

"I'm not flattering you, Hetty. I am genuinely grateful for what you've done for my daughter." Blair truly was, too. There had been nowhere else he could have sent his daughter when his business troubles began.

Unplacated, Hetty marched up the carpet and back again, looking as though she wanted to toss Blair out the window.

"The truth is, Blair, it was my intention never to speak a word to you again. Unfortunately, uh, circumstance has prevented that."

Hoping to make his exit before more hot words erupted, Blair edged away from the sofa. He hadn't forgotten the episode at the funeral and knew what Hetty was capable of when she really got worked up.

"That is unfortunate...for both of us."

Hetty had no intention of letting Blair escape so easily. Drawing herself up, she attacked the main issue head on.

"Am I to assume, then, that you're here to take Sara?" she demanded with a voice frigid enough to freeze the tea in the pot.

"Yes."

There was no point in hedging about the matter now. Blair only stated the stark, bald truth.

Something like panic struck Hetty, though she quickly covered it. She had taken in her sister's child, been a mother to her and grown deeply attached to her. Now this man expected to waltz into Rose Cottage at will and hustle the child away. Well, now this man had Hetty King to deal with! As always, when pushed into a corner, Hetty came out fighting. She clenched her fists and planted herself firmly in front of Blair.

"How foolish of me to think otherwise, knowing you as I do. True to form, you dropped her on us when it was convenient for you, and now I suppose it's convenient for you to take her away?"

Blair was not used to being talked to that way, and his craggy face tensed.

"I don't think this is the kind of conversation we should be having in front of Sara," he muttered stiffly.

To emphasize the point, he stalked out into the front hall. Olivia, ever the peacemaker, pursued him.

"Blair, please," she pleaded helplessly.

Peace seemed pretty much a long shot right then. Hetty, bent on recriminations, sped in Blair's wake. She caught him pulling on his boots and closed in for combat.

"Admit it, Blair, Sara stands a better chance of growing up a normal, healthy child in Avonlea than ever she would in that pampered little world of yours in Montreal. Oh, she goes to a proper school here. She's got color in her cheeks. She managed without a nursemaid catering to her every whim."

This was rapidly becoming a case of an irresistible force meeting an immovable object. Blair

gritted his teeth, almost yanked a hook off his
overshoe, but still clung to his self-control.

"Please, Hetty, I am her father, and you won't
find me as easy to dispatch as Sara's Nanny
Louisa."

As calmly as he could, Blair was asserting his
rights as a parent, rights Hetty had become
accustomed to thinking of as her own. Blair
might as well have issued a direct challenge with
trumpet and gauntlet. Hetty began to quiver all
over.

"I want you out of the house immediately."

Blair nodded. The last place he wanted to be
trapped now was in Rose Cottage with Hetty in a
rage.

"Gladly. Please have Sara ready to leave
tomorrow at nine a.m. sharp."

He turned to find Olivia and Sara standing
horror-stricken in the doorway of the parlor.

"Blair, please," Olivia tried again.

"I'm truly sorry, Olivia," Blair said to her,
kindly but firmly.

Sara, too, made a beseeching gesture. She had
been so sure that a nice cup of tea and a chat at
Rose Cottage would change his mind. How could
she ever have imagined such a fracas would
ensue? Now she saw her father was deadly serious about getting on the train with her tomorrow.

"Papa..."

"Don't worry, sweetheart, it'll be all right. I'll be staying with Janet and Alec, and I'll see you in the morning."

With that, Blair kissed Sara goodbye and tramped out the door without so much as a backward glance at Hetty. Olivia remained standing, rigid with shock. Sara burst into tears and rushed as fast as she could up the stairs to her room. Hetty winced at the slam of Sara's door and turned her ire upon Olivia.

"Olivia, I hold you responsible for all of this. I cannot believe you would be so senseless and—and thoughtless as to allow that man in this house in the first place."

At this totally irrational accusation, Olivia flushed a violent red. She couldn't see what difference being inside or outside of Rose Cottage would have made to Blair's decision.

"I was just being courteous, Hetty. Blair is family, after all."

And with this, Olivia, too, bolted upstairs, leaving Hetty to contemplate the total ruin of the afternoon.

Chapter Six

Darkness came early at this time of year. At the King farmhouse, Janet King, carrying a folded blanket over her arm, opened the door to peer out into the night. Behind her, Alec stood adjusting an oil lamp.

"Where is that man?" Janet frowned. "I can't imagine him wanting to spend *that* much time with Hetty."

Alec couldn't imagine it either. Long ago he had learned that, with Hetty, prudent discretion was by far the safest course of action. Though he, too, had a lot of misgivings about what would happen when Blair and Hetty met, he kept them to himself.

"Janet, I think we should stay out of the situation as much as possible."

Janet shook her head. She had a far more excitable nature than her husband and often got frustrated with his tolerant attitudes.

"Oh, Alec, that's what you always say."

"Yes," Alec grinned, "so it shouldn't come as any surprise." Alec's calm head and refusal to meddle had defused many a tense situation before this. He just hoped Blair managed to escape Avonlea in one piece after Hetty was done with him.

Thinking they were alone in their conversation, the two turned back towards the kitchen. But they most certainly weren't alone. At the top of the front stairs, just above their heads, every child in the King house was hanging over the stair rail trying to overhear as much as possible. With the possibility of Sara being taken away in the morning, none of them had been able to even think about sleep. They all wanted desperately for Sara to stay and were practically burning up to find out if any of the adults had managed to bring about a change of plans. As soon as Alec and Janet disappeared, they straightened swiftly.

"Kitchen stairs," Felix whispered into Felicity's ear.

Felix led the way, with Felicity, Andrew and Cecily at his heels. Inside of a minute, they were all crowded onto the landing of the kitchen stairs, a prime listening post for anything that went on below.

"Blair is Sara's father," Alec was saying to Janet as they walked back into the circle of warmth radiating from the big kitchen stove. "I mean, he was going to come for her sooner or later."

Janet had to admit this point, though she wasn't happy about it. No one had had any idea what was going to happen at Blair's trial, making Sara's future quite uncertain. And Sara had fitted in so well that everyone had just given up remembering that her real home wasn't in Avonlea.

Distractedly, Janet began taking down the socks that were drying in a row over the heat of the stove. Janet felt strongly about warm winter socks and would have had a fit had she known about all the little bare feet on the chilly floors upstairs.

"Yes, well, I just don't think it's fair to uproot her so suddenly."

Alec began taking socks from his wife, who was quickly acquiring an armful and not thinking about where she was going to put them. With six people in the house, socks went through the laundry at an enormous rate.

"You know what I think?" muttered Janet tartly. "Blair is not thinking of Sara. He's thinking only of himself."

Alec spotted the wicker laundry basket and tossed the socks into it.

"Ah...it seems I'm one of the few members of this family who is not an expert on what other people are thinking."

The grown-ups were too absorbed in their own conversation to hear the tiny creaks and shiftings made by the children as they tried to keep still on the squeaky boards.

Janet refused to be diverted from her line of logic. She would have to deal with all the upsets after Blair and Sara were gone. "Oh, if only we could make him stay a little longer. At least, oh, Alec, the children are going to miss her so much. I'm going to miss her."

Alec rubbed his chin, just then realizing how much Sara Stanley had insinuated her way into all their hearts. He was so used to seeing her in the kitchen that she might as well have been one of his own children. There was always some new project or escapade afoot when Sara was around. And she had certainly livened up prim Felicity.

"I know. I will too."

"Couldn't you talk some sense into him?"

In spite of Janet's appeal, they both knew this was a farfetched notion. Blair hadn't become as successful as he was by being easily diverted from his purpose.

"What can I say? You know Blair—once he's made his mind up, you can move land and sea— he won't budge."

And there was a lot of Blair Stanley in his daughter. Everyone had discovered that when she went on a hunger strike almost as soon as she had arrived in Avonlea, over Nanny Louisa being sent away.

Janet had just opened her mouth for another try at persuading Alec when she was cut short by the sound of the front door banging shut. She looked at her husband in alarm.

"Oh, he's back."

In trepidation, Alec and Janet headed back to the hall to see what condition Hetty had sent Blair back in. Above their heads, there was a rush of young feet as all the children hurried to the front stairs in an effort to keep up with the situation. Blair had stomped in, furious, slamming the door behind him without any regard as to who might be in bed sleeping. He was shucking himself out of his overcoat when Alec and Janet appeared.

"That woman! I don't care if she is your sister. Roasting in hell would be preferable to dealing with her!"

Janet almost dropped the sock she was holding.

"Blair, shhh! You'll wake the children." And teach them words they had no business knowing!

Stiffly, Alec and Janet retreated to the kitchen, followed by Blair. This precipitated another stampede back to the kitchen stairs by the unsuspected listeners above. Listeners who wished heartily that the grown-ups would make up their minds about staying in one place.

In the kitchen, Blair flung himself down in one

of the kitchen chairs. His face was mottled scarlet and the muscles at his jaw were tight as steel. Blair Stanley was not a man used to being crossed.

"What is wrong with her narrow little mind? That woman has a chip on her shoulder and I would like to knock it off with a—"

"Things didn't go well with Hetty?" Janet concluded hastily before Blair's growlings could become any more hair-raising. "Oh, well, I suppose you two gentlemen have a lot to talk about, don't you Alec? So I'll just go upstairs and make sure the children are all settled in. Blair, I've put you in the girls' room. They're going to bunk in with the boys."

Shooting a significant glance at her husband, Janet started towards the back stairs.

Still hot over Hetty, Blair nodded curtly. Janet beat a hasty retreat before she could be drawn in any more deeply than she already was. The children, who had just got themselves nicely settled at the top of the kitchen stairs, heard their mother's step and jumped up.

"Uh-oh, run," whispered Cecily, standing frozen nevertheless. Felix gave her a quick poke.

"Go, Cecily!"

Nightshirts flying, the children scampered

away, leaving the stair landing in innocent empti-
ness by the time Janet began to make her way
upward.

With Janet's defection, Alec found himself left
alone with Blair Stanley and the family strife. He
speedily assessed Blair's state of mind and
decided upon his own form of tonic.

"You look like a man who could use some for-
tification."

Pulling over a kitchen chair, Alec climbed up
onto it and felt around on the very top of the
kitchen cabinet. With a little grunt, he found what
he was looking for and got back down. The bottle
he set on the table was dark, with a fading label
and a distinctly forbidden look.

And no wonder! The bottle was a brandy
bottle, an outrageous possession in teetotal
Avonlea. Alec turned it over in his hand.

"Now, this is, uh, strictly for medicinal pur-
poses, of course," he told Blair with a wink.

"Of course."

Blair's lip curled with the first hint of humor
he had shown since he stormed in. The sight of a
King ferreting out a bottle of brandy wasn't one
he was going to see very often in his lifetime.

Taking the precaution of using teacups, Alec
poured out a drink for himself and for Blair. He
stared at the bottle thoughtfully.

"You know, I don't think I've had a drink of this since...since Cecily was born."

"Really?" Blair drawled unbelievingly.

"Well..." Alec chuckled, "maybe once or twice since then."

Relieved that some of the tension was lifting, Alec slid one of the cups towards his guest. Somewhat mollified, Blair picked it up. With an air of being men of the world, the two clinked rims over the sugar bowl.

"Cheers," they toasted, in carefully low voices that wouldn't travel up the stairs to Janet whom they could hear moving around above their heads. Keeping an eye on the kitchen stairs, they each took a cautious sip.

Chapter Seven

Back in Rose Cottage, everything was in a turmoil. The tea sat, stone cold, in the teapot in the parlor. Sara had fled to her room, with Olivia close behind her, and Hetty stormed up and down the parlor alone, with no one to vent her anger on.

Olivia was worried about Sara, for the sight of Sara in tears was a rare one around Rose Cottage.

Quietly, Olivia padded down the hall, hesitated outside Sara's door and finally knocked.

"Come in," said a thin voice from inside.

Olivia, who hated scenes, pushed the door open and glided inside, afraid of what she might find. She discovered Sara engaged in packing her bags. Dresses were laid out on chairs, the big wardrobe in the corner of the room yawned open, and the drawers of the bureau revealed camisoles and petticoats spilling over the edge. The sight filled Olivia with instant chagrin. The open suitcases brought home reality in a way all Blair's and Hetty's words had been unable to. It really was true! Sara would be gone from Rose Cottage in the morning!

"Sara, you should be in bed by now. You can finish packing in the morning," Olivia gently told her.

Sara kept right on stuffing items into her luggage. Sleep was the furthest thing from her mind. Within the last few hours she'd been tossed up and down on such a roller coaster of happiness and dismay that she felt she might not be interested in sleeping again for weeks to come.

"Why do Aunt Hetty and Papa hate each other so much?" she demanded of Olivia, at the same time trying to fold her best cream dress with all the tucks down the front and edgings of lace. She had worn that very dress when she had given the narration at the Avonlea magic lantern show. The show had been a triumph, winning the admiration of the people of Avonlea and drawing Jasper Dale out of seclusion to run the projector. It was mainly because of that show, which Sara had organized, that Jasper had got up the courage to be Olivia's photographer and...oh, why was everything so suddenly all mixed up?

Sara flung the dress down on the bedspread and turned to Olivia, confused by the mysteries of adult behavior and pained at having two of the people most dear to her at loggerheads. Olivia sucked in a deep breath and tried to explain.

"Oh, it's senseless, Sara. Hetty blames him for taking your mother away from us, and some people just can't let go of a hurt. Seems like the longer they hold onto it, the larger it becomes."

This explanation didn't hold out a lot of hope for improving matters. Both Sara and Olivia knew that Hetty was a woman of unbending principles and even more unbending willpower. Once Hetty made up her mind about something, it was practically impossible to make her change it—a characteristic that had caused more than a few storms at Rose Cottage. Very clearly, Sara saw what it all could mean. For all her youth, Sara often had extraordinary insights into other people's character.

"If we leave tomorrow, then they'll always hate each other, forever."

The last word echoed through the room as dolefully as a funeral bell, and Olivia could not disagree. Her bosom heaved with a sigh.

"Well, there are some things you just can't change, Sara."

This wasn't exactly the sort of comfort Sara had hoped for from Olivia. It wasn't very reassuring to have one's grown-up aunt as much as saying things were hopeless.

"I'm frightened, Aunt Olivia," Sara got out, her voice small and her eyes huge with everything Rose Cottage had come to mean to her. "I'm frightened that if we leave tomorrow, I'll never be able to come back here."

Olivia enfolded Sara in a big hug, unable to say out loud that she was afraid of the same thing.

"Oh, Sara, you can always come back here, whenever you want...even if I have to go to Montreal and get you."

"It wouldn't be the same, though," Sara murmured mournfully against Olivia's shoulder. "I'd just be a visitor, and visitors never get treated the same as real family."

Hetty began to quiver all over. "I want you
out of the house immediately."
"Gladly. Please have Sara ready to leave tomorrow
at nine a.m. sharp."

❧

"I'm frightened, Aunt Olivia," Sara got out,
her voice small and her eyes huge with
everything Rose Cottage had come to mean to her.
"I'm frightened that if we leave tomorrow,
I'll never be able to come back here."

⟲⟳⟲⟳

Jasper stopped cold as Olivia's words sank in.
"Run away?" Olivia nodded, biting her lips.
"Her father came to take her home,
and she didn't want to leave."

⟲⟳⟲⟳

Hetty screwed up the napkin, flung it down
and burst into tears. "I know, Olivia. I know it.
Now I've lost Sara. I should never have
stood in Blair Stanley's way. I'm losing you, too."

❧❧❧

Before Hetty could resist, Alec had her by the arm
and up on the ice. Ignoring her squawks,
he swung her round on the slick surface,
laughing heartily.

Olivia embraced Sara even more tightly. Her own heart was swelling up so much she felt it in danger of bursting her bodice buttons. With Hetty ruling the household with such an iron hand, Olivia sometimes felt as young as Sara. And it was as though, in Sara, she had gained a very dear little sister instead of just a niece.

"I promise...that will never happen," Olivia pledged vehemently. "Our feelings for you will never change, no matter where you are."

Down the lane from Rose Cottage, in the King kitchen, Alec and Blair had pretty well consumed the brandy in the teacups. Blair had calmed down and been restored, at least temporarily, to rational conversation. Man to man, he set about describing his affairs to his brother-in-law.

"I still have controlling interest in the company," he said, explaining what he had salvaged from the financial disaster brought on by his fraudulent partner. "And I've managed to hold on to the house."

It was just like Blair to bounce back from the fiasco and come out fighting. Blair was a self-made man. And, like most self-made men, he was given to bold, decisive action, blithely taking on all odds in order to succeed. It had been this dashing side of him that had laid siege to Ruth King and swept her off her feet. It was this side of him that made him assume he could just hustle Sara back to her former life without any consequences. And it was this side of him that roused Hetty to battle.

He had made himself rich once before and, from the determined glint in his eyes, it was clear he meant to recover from his setback and make himself rich once again. And he wanted to get started on the process as soon as possible.

Alec nodded sagely, as though Blair's world of high finance and fast-moving international business deals were quite as familiar to him as his own barnyard. Why, a few more sips of brandy and he might start thinking of taking up high finance himself.

"Ah...well, if you need help, we've put a little aside, and if you can use it, it's there for you and Sara."

It was as natural as breathing for the King clan to stick together and try to help each other. Blair was moved but too proud even to consider the offer.

"Thank you, Alec, that's very kind, but I have every intention of building the company back up, and that's another reason why I want to get back to Montreal as soon as possible."

This statement got them right back to the main problem: the sudden and totally unexpected uprooting of Sara from what she had come to regard as her home. Janet had charged Alec with doing something about it and he knew he had better try soon or he might never hear the end of it from his wife. Clearing his throat, Alec decided upon a cautiously diplomatic, slantwise approach.

"Now, if you don't mind my saying, you know, courtrooms give a man a certain pallor. You'd do yourself a lot of good to stay here for a few days, let the Island rejuvenate you. Well, I can help smooth things over with Hetty," he offered recklessly—no doubt under the influence of the brandy. "But, uh...you got to give Sara some time. She's got a lot of farewells to make."

The only result of this speech was to make Blair resolute again.

"I'm sorry. I've agonized over this...and I believe it's for the best."

A quick, short chop of the ties, that's what Blair believed would be the least painful. Besides, it would quickly get him out of range of Hetty King. From the first day he had shown up to court Ruth, Hetty had been the thorn among the roses. She had never liked him or accepted him.

From the recent explosion at Rose Cottage, he was certain she never would.

Alec supposed he ought to argue some more, but, with Blair's mind so adamantly made up, he couldn't think of anything further to say. All he could do was lift one hand in a conciliating gesture.

"All right, I won't say another word."

Good thing too, for footsteps creaked on the kitchen stairs and Janet's voice floated down.

"Alec?"

"Whoops!"

The brandy bottle! If Janet suspected he and Blair had been sitting here drinking, he knew he'd never hear the end of it. Grabbing up the incriminating evidence, Alec scrambled onto the chair again, almost dropping the bottle twice before shoving it back atop the cupboard into its hiding place. Luck was with him, however. When Janet returned to the kitchen, she found the two sitting innocuously at the table before a pair of empty teacups.

"Alec...oh, Blair—well, your room's all ready for you, and I've put out some fresh towels." Janet had taken a deliberately long time upstairs in order to give the men time to talk. Now all she wanted was to get the details from Alec.

"Thank you," Blair said, discovering again

that family hospitality was always better than the finest hotel. "I certainly hope I haven't put you out, Janet—or the children."

Janet waved her hand airily.

"Oh, no. The four of them are quite comfortable. I think it's a bit of an adventure."

"Well, goodnight, then," said Blair, getting to his feet. "And thank you for the, um...advice, Alec."

"Any time, Blair."

Wearier from the tensions of the day than he wanted to admit, Blair took himself up the stairs. Janet waited until he was out of earshot and then turned eagerly to her husband, whose calm expression she misinterpreted completely.

"Good for you. So he did listen," she declared with satisfaction.

"Listen?" Alec dragged his attention abruptly from the depths of the empty teacup. "Oh, well, no..."

"What?"

"He's still planning on leaving first thing in the morning," Alec informed her, bracing himself.

At once, Janet became agitated again. She tugged at her apron, did a half-turn around the kitchen table, then stopped beside the chair Blair had vacated, fortunately not catching the pungent scent rising from the cup left behind.

"Oh...then Hetty's the problem," she muttered, approaching the matter from yet another angle. "You've got to talk to Hetty, Alec. It's the only way to straighten this out."

Hurriedly remembering it was his bedtime too, Alec rose up from the table. In hopes of getting hazardous ideas out of Janet's mind, he patted her arm.

"Janet, calm down! It's late. I'm tired."

Alec's voice inadvertently covered the commotion upstairs. The minute Blair had disappeared into his room and the coast was clear, all the children had leaped out of bed again and swarmed back to the top of the stairs. It had been torture, lying still and faking sleep while Janet had puttered around, tucking in the covers and folding clothes. Not only that, they had missed all the conversation between Blair and Alec, and now they had a ton of stuff to get caught up on.

The children no sooner got themselves settled behind the newel post than Alec headed for the front hall, Janet at his heels. Suppressing groans, the children all got up again and crept as fast as they could along the hall to the front stairs where they knelt against the railing.

All Alec wanted to do was escape to bed, but his wife was having none of it. It was perfectly clear to her, if to no one else, that if things weren't smoothed out very soon, Sara would be gone—and then where would they be? To prevent a permanent rupture in the family, she set her mouth and turned up the pressure on Alec.

"Oh, well, I don't know Alec," she sighed. "I used to think I'd married the head of the family, but now I'm beginning to wonder who does wear the trousers on this farm—you or Hetty."

"There's a time and place for everything, dear," Alec returned, as mildly as he could, as he put his foot on the bottom stair. "I'll go over in the morning."

"In the morning!" Any fool could see that any action in the morning would be too little too late, "Sara will be gone. Go over now and tell Hetty what you think."

Alec grasped the stair rail, listening to the cold wind blowing about outside.

"I'm not going to go over to Rose Cottage to rant and rave at Hetty at this hour."

"Why not?" Janet wanted to know. "Unless, of course, you're still afraid of Hetty."

There really was going to be no end to this unless Alec did what Janet wanted. Defeated, he threw up his hands in exasperation and reached for his overcoat.

Chapter Eight

When Olivia emerged from Sara's room at Rose Cottage, her face was white as the piano keys in the parlor and her mouth quivering. Sara really was leaving. By this time tomorrow, the little room at the top of the stairs would be empty and silent. No youthful laughter would dance through the kitchen, no rushing steps would echo in the hall. Oh, if only she could have had some warning, just a little time to adjust to the jarring change about to befall her home.

Assaulted by a hundred disheartening thoughts, Olivia turned and all but ran into Hetty, who had finally come up the stairs too. After the scene inside Sara's room, mild Olivia was ready to tackle even her formidable older sister. She stepped squarely in front of her in the upstairs hall, the lamp she was carrying trembling in her hand.

"Hetty, how could you have said all those things to Blair with Sara standing right there? The poor child was so upset I could barely get her settled down."

When it came to handing out blame, Hetty was no slacker herself. She immediately bristled all over.

"If you'd listened to me, Olivia, this would never have happened. Give me that." The oil lamp shook so alarmingly that it looked in danger of tumbling to the floor, and Hetty took it from Olivia. "But, as usual, you didn't think before you opened your mouth."

Usually a strong word or two from Hetty would put Olivia in her place, but not this time. Her shoulders quivered as her breath came faster. She didn't see how failing to invite Blair inside would have changed anything.

"No, Hetty, you're the one who didn't think. You've done the very thing that will ensure Sara leaves the Island tomorrow."

Hetty flung a glance at Sara's door.

"Oh, shhh!" she ordered, very belatedly taking a care for what Sara overheard. "You'd no right to allow that man to set foot in my house."

With Olivia blocking the hall, Hetty turned on her heel and started down the stairs again, signifying that the conversation was at an end. Olivia stared after her, let out a little gasp and set off in hot pursuit. This was one time when she was having none of Hetty's head-of-the-household ways.

Behind them, Sara tiptoed out of her room and peered after their retreating backs. Now not only were her father and her Aunt Hetty fighting, but her Aunt Hetty and her Aunt Olivia were snarling at each other like cats on a barbed-wire fence. Her young face crumpled up as she tiptoed to the landing to watch.

There was plenty to see. Olivia, perfectly rigid, managed to contain herself only until they got to the bottom of the stairs.

"Your house?" she exploded when her foot hit the ground floor.

"Well, I'm the eldest," Hetty shot back, caught completely off balance by Olivia's outburst. What was worse, Olivia showed absolutely no sign of going back to her old, meek self.

"Oh," Olivia seethed, pointing to the hall rug, "and is this your carpet? Is this your lamp? Is nothing mine? Then perhaps it would be best if I left, too."

Aghast, Hetty stared at her sister. "Don't be ridiculous," she sputtered, supposing that Olivia was not only impertinent but well on her way to losing her mind.

"You needn't continue to support me," Olivia plunged on madly. "I'm perfectly capable of being independent now that I'm earning some money of my own."

So far, Hetty gathered, Olivia had earned only enough to squander on a new hat—which she had flaunted in an effort to impress that bungling photographer of hers, Jasper Dale. Hetty's jaw shot out. She could be pushed only so far, even by an angry Olivia.

"Yes? And just what would you do? Where would you go?"

This wasn't a possibility Olivia had ever thought about before, but she wasn't about to be bested by Hetty now.

"I could...take a room at the boarding house," she improvised, not caring that the idea of Olivia King moving into the boarding house would keep Avonlea in gossip for a year.

"Ho, well, that's just as ludicrous as saying you'd...you'd elope with Jasper Dale!"

Hetty didn't even have time to regret planting such a dangerous notion in Olivia's head before a sharp rap rattled the front door. Both women started, again endangering the lamp. Mightily surprised, they blinked at the grandfather clock in the corner. Who could be calling at such an hour?

Hetty opened the door with a jerk to find her brother standing there, bundled haphazardly into his overcoat and looking very disgruntled indeed.

"I'm sorry," he began, "but I can't sleep until I've told you what's on my mind."

With that, he pushed his way into the warmth of the kitchen, bringing a gust of icy air with him and leaving his sisters no choice but to follow. Just as her cousins, Sara then crept halfway down the stairs and pressed her face against the railing to listen.

In the kitchen, Alec stuffed his mitts into his pocket and ploughed straight into his mission.

"I want you to know, Hetty, that I have stood by once too often while you...overstepped all the bounds of common decency."

Hetty, who considered herself the very arbiter of common decency in Avonlea, let out a yelp.

"Has everyone gone mad?" she demanded of the air above her head.

Alec refused to be deterred by her dramatics.

"Look." He gritted his teeth. "You've made your own bed. You can lie in it, for all I care, but not where that child is concerned. I can't tolerate any more of these disruptive partings."

Hetty grew redder and more ruffled with each of Alec's words. Mature head of a family he might be, but to Hetty, he was still her younger brother who ought to do what he was told. Tonight, both he and Olivia seemed to have kicked over the traces completely.

"I don't know what you're talking about," Hetty rapped out, looking ferociously severe. The lamplight played on her sharp cheekbones and long nose, making her appear even more intimidating.

Alec ran his fingers distractedly through his hair. He didn't know why he had ever expected Hetty to listen to reason.

"I'm telling you, Hetty, if what Blair said to me tonight is any indication in all probability, you will never, ever see Sara again."

In the shadowy stairway, Sara almost gasped aloud. It had been bad enough to suffer all the discord among her relatives. It had been bad enough to have to leave her beloved Rose Cottage on scarcely a day's notice and expect to come back only as a guest. But never to come back at all! Why, Sara felt petrified to her bones at the very possibility.

The threat horrified Olivia almost as much as it did Sara. She threw her weight on Alec's side.

"Hetty, please," she pleaded, "make your peace with him once and for all. You're the only one who can change things."

Flexibility was not Hetty's strong suit, especially when she was feeling cornered and under assault. Her brows flew stormily together.

"So you both want me to make my peace with Blair Stanley, even though he's about to take away Sara, just as he did our Ruth? That's what you want me to do, is it?"

"Yes," declared Alec bluntly, oblivious to the fact that Sara was sitting on the stairs on the verge of tears. Blair held all the cards here. Making peace with him seemed the only course to take.

"Over my dead body," was Hetty's reply, and she looked very much as though she meant that literally. The situation was Blair's fault, and there was no way Hetty was going to admit otherwise.

Hetty stalked from the room, leaving Alec to clench his fists and Olivia with no idea what to do or say.

"Good Lord, woman!" Alec spluttered after her. He flung down his hat in disgust.

Hearing Hetty's footsteps, Sara flew to her room. The last thing she needed at the end of this most crazy day was to be caught on the stairs listening to fights. Jumping headlong into bed, she shut her eyes tight as Hetty opened the door to peep in.

Dresses and pinafores still lay scattered where Olivia had persuaded Sara to abandon them. The suitcases still stood open, as did the wardrobe in the corner. Hetty might have been furious when she opened the door, but all the signs of packing jolted her just as much as they had Olivia.

Thinking herself unobserved, she stood stock-still, the anger draining away, to be replaced by a pained and somber gloom. Her gaze lingered on Sara for what seemed an endless moment, remembering another fair-haired girl who had slept in that room and been wooed away forever by a rich city man. Then, satisfied the child was asleep, Hetty sighed heavily, stepped back into the hall and quietly closed the door behind her.

The older woman had not been unobserved. Sara, through half-closed lashes, had seen everything and her Aunt Hetty's face had proved the last straw. Sara's spirit was roused. With her whole world falling down around her ears, it sure wasn't going to do any good spending the night sniffling into her pillow. If anything concrete was going to be done to solve the situation, she'd just have to do it herself.

The minute the door was shut, Sara leaped out of bed again and began flinging on her clothes. When in a fix, Sara believed in action, no matter how fantastic. A desperate situation called for a desperate plan, and Sara had hit upon just such a plan the instant her Aunt Hetty had turned away. She ran down the stairs and peeped into the kitchen just in time to see her Uncle Alec retrieve his hat from the floor and cram it down around his ears.

"Aw, Hetty will never change," he was grumbling at Olivia by way of goodnight. "Blair's just as stubborn. Thank goodness Sara has some sense. Maybe some of it will rub off on them."

He might quickly have revised his opinion about Sara's store of sense had he known the wild scheme she was putting into action at that very moment. Before either of her relatives could see her, Sara pulled on her hat and coat and slipped out the front door.

A short while later, after a wind-buffeted race through the winter dark, and after her Uncle Alec was safely inside, Sara dragged a heavy ladder against the side of the King farmhouse. She then proceeded to climb the teetering thing up to the second story and tap on the window of the room where she knew her cousins were asleep.

And asleep they were, sound asleep, quite worn out from the day's events and all the scurrying about in the dark. Felicity and Cecily lay bundled up under quilts in one bed, Felix and Andrew in the other. Sara thought she was going to have to rattle the window right out of its frame before any of them stirred.

Andrew, being the lightest sleeper, was the one who finally sat up abruptly and rubbed at his eyes. Could that possibly be a person waving out-side the glass twenty feet above the earth?

Since Andrew didn't believe what his eyes were seeing, he got up out of bed, padded across the floor and opened the window. Only then did he accept that he wasn't dreaming.

"Sara!" he croaked, seeing her apparently sus-pended in midair against the side of the house.

"Help me inside," Sara commanded, shivering in the night wind and swaying on the ladder which, truth to tell, she hadn't bothered to plant very firmly at the bottom.

Andrew obliged by gripping her arms and starting to drag her inside, bumping her hipbones over the sill.

"You're hurting me," Sara protested as she wriggled forward with Andrew's help and then tumbled into the room. Her shrill voice was loud enough to wake the others in the room.

"What are you doing here?" Andrew wanted to know as he helped her to her feet and quickly shut the window against the whistling breeze.

"Cecily, Sara's here," Felicity whispered to her little sister, who was blinking in bewilderment at the dim figures by the window. Cecily was just as likely to believe a ghost had got in and squawk loud enough to bring their mother running.

Cecily's eyes popped wide. It really was Sara. And Sara certainly hadn't arrived by way of the door.

"Have you run away?" she asked breathlessly.

By this time, Felix had got himself out from under the quilt. "What's going on?" he mumbled drowsily. Felix always took a long time to get fully awake.

Sara took a deep breath to compose herself and faced them all.

"I've decided that I'm not going to leave until Aunt Hetty and Papa make up. Otherwise, I'll never be able to come back here."

Andrew shook his head. Andrew was a quiet, intellectual boy who lacked Sara's streak of imaginative boldness.

"You're leaving all right. You should have heard your father tonight."

"He was so mad at Aunt Hetty I thought his veins were gonna explode," Felix added dramatically. Though Felix hated to see Sara go, part of him was secretly enjoying the fireworks going off around him.

"I don't care," flung out Sara in the face of this ominous fact. "I'm not leaving."

Cecily, too young to see the real complications involved, brightened at once.

"Oh, good, Sara. I don't want you to go."

Felicity, who would have been shocked at such an idea only months ago, now found herself falling in readily with Sara.

"Well, you're going to have to disappear."

"Where do you suggest we hide you?" Andrew joked. "Under the bed?"

When Sara didn't even smile at this, they saw she was indeed serious. And if they didn't help her, who knew what trouble she'd get into on her own? Sara could be a bit of a hothead, but if she didn't always look before she leaped, at least she was brave enough to leap in the first place. And she was very sporting about landing in heaps of thorns.

"I know the perfect place," Felicity said, in a sudden flash of inspiration.

"They'll be so remorseful," Sara muttered, thinking of all the people she had seen fighting recently. "They'll have to forget about their quarrel...and unite in their love for me."

"Yech!" was Felix's comment on that rosy picture.

Sara merely turned to the bed, glorying in the thought of making everyone beg humble forgiveness for their wrongheaded actions of today.

"I think it's a wonderful idea."

Chapter Nine

No one slept at Rose Cottage that night. Olivia tossed and turned in a fever of restlessness, imagining herself installed in a freezing attic at the Biggins' boarding house and Hetty never speaking to her again. Hetty lay perfectly rigid, staring at the ceiling, wondering why the rest of the family never saw eye to eye with her but always had to be contrary. And Sara...well, Sara wasn't even there at all.

It was Hetty who got up first, and Hetty who discovered Sara's empty bed. The sight gave Hetty a terrible fright. Still wearing her night-clothes, she called hastily to Olivia.

"Has Sara been up already this morning?" she demanded when Olivia emerged, puffy-eyed, from her room.

"I don't think so. Why?" Olivia asked. Then she caught sight of Sara's empty bed through the door. "Oh, gracious Providence," she groaned, immediately imagining the worst.

"This is all the fault of that—blasted Blair Stanley," Hetty exploded as she hurried to get dressed. According to Hetty, the arrival of Blair Stanley was becoming equivalent to the Black Plague and a couple of earthquakes all rolled into one.

A short while later, Hetty came bustling into the kitchen, at the same time trying to fasten her earring. No matter what disaster befell, Hetty always made sure she met it properly turned out. It was a matter of moral principle. Once you let your moral principles down everything else would fall into wrack and ruin.

"Peter! Peter!" she called out impatiently.

Peter Craig, the hired boy at Rose Cottage, sped in the back door from outside. His hair was falling down over his eyes and he looked considerably shaken up. Sara was *his* friend, too. She had helped him when he was sick and made the Kings, especially Felicity, treat him like a friend instead of just a hired boy. His first shock that morning had been when Hetty routed him out of bed and told him that Sara was missing. His second shock had been to learn from Olivia that when Sara was found, she was going to leave Rose Cottage for good anyway, maybe without even time to say goodbye.

"She's nowhere. I checked in the shed, the chicken coop, everywhere."

"Well, did you look under the house?"

"Uh, no, ma'am," Peter admitted, unable to imagine Sara hunched in the crawl space under the porch.

"Well, then, do so. Go on."

In her anxiety about Sara, Hetty pushed Peter out the back door again. Like Blair, Hetty was a person of activity and command, and it made her feel better to be able take charge of the search. As soon as Peter was gone, Olivia rushed in from the hall bearing more unwelcome news.

"Hetty! Blair's here."

Beleaguered on all fronts, Hetty spun round.

"Oh! Oh! Good Lord!"

"This can't be happening!" Olivia added, in bald contradiction of the facts. Wringing her hands, she rushed back out again.

Olivia kept right on rushing until she was through the front door and out beside the buggy from which Blair and Alec were just descending. Neither man knew about Sara's disappearance yet, and they were calmly expecting to pick her up.

"Blair!" Olivia cried.

"Morning, Olivia."

"Um, Blair, we have a slight delay. Um, we don't quite know..."

As Olivia's voice trailed off, Blair snapped instantly to attention. He hadn't expected Hetty to give up easily, and he was ready for any countering maneuver on her part.

"Well, she is ready, isn't she? Then I'll go up and bring her things down."

Seeing Olivia standing there, speechless, Hetty swept out through the door. There was no point in putting off the news any longer.

"Sara isn't upstairs, Blair," Hetty said grimly. "She's—she's gone."

"Gone," cried Blair in amazement. "What in blazes do you mean, gone?"

"She's gone!" Olivia confirmed, standing out in the chill air without so much as a shawl. "We went to wake her up this morning, and she wasn't there."

Without waiting for another word, Blair raced inside Rose Cottage to see for himself.

"Sara," he called out, opening the parlor door, "Sara!"

When Sara didn't materialize from behind the sofa or the piano, he turned hotly upon Hetty, who had followed him back in.

"Hetty King, I can't believe the lengths to which you'd go. Where have you hidden her?"

He barreled out of the parlor, all but knocking Hetty over in the process. Hetty swelled up in outrage.

"Hidden? What kind of a woman do you think I am?"

"Don't ask me," Blair ground out. "Sara!"

He clattered up the stairs and began flinging

open doors on the second floor, seeming to think that the more noise he made the sooner Sara would appear.

Alec clomped up onto the porch with Olivia. He was doing his best to keep a cooler head.

"Look, how could she..."

"Alec, I don't know. Maybe she went over to your house to say goodbye."

Alec shook his head as they stepped into the front hall.

"We just came from there, Olivia." There was no way Sara could have trotted across the fields to the King farm without being seen from the buggy.

While Blair was tramping around Sara's room, Peter Craig ran back into the kitchen, where he found Hetty glaring up towards the racket Blair was making. Peter was now covered all over with dust and bits of dead grass from crawling about on his searches. He had looked even under the ivy trellis where the cat refused to go.

"She's not anywhere, Miss King."

If she wasn't at the King farm and she wasn't under the house, matters were serious. It was time to call in outside help.

"Oh, please go for Constable Jeffries, Peter."

As Peter galloped off on this new errand, Blair came back down the stairs, running into Alec and Olivia below.

"Damn it, she is gone," fumed Blair, flinging looks of black suspicion toward Hetty.

"I told you she was," Hetty snorted, as much as implying that Blair was of limited intelligence and doubtful understanding.

This was too much. Blair twitched with fury and finally lost control.

"Don't you say another word to me, you old battle-ax. You ought to be tarred and feathered."

Alec and Olivia looked perfectly stunned— which was nothing at all to the expression on Hetty's face. No one had dared speak to her this way within living memory.

"Blair, that's enough," barked Alec. "Let's start looking."

"I'm right behind you."

Alec hustled Blair out the front door before more torpedoes could be launched. Hetty stood staring after Blair with fiery eyes, then sprang into life herself. Like Blair, she felt she had to be doing something.

"Don't stand there ogling, Olivia. Start looking."

Olivia was already pulling on her own coat, although where she intended to look she had no idea. She only knew she was becoming thoroughly provoked with her sister.

"If you would just calm down and come to

your senses, Hetty, we'd all stand a better chance of finding Sara!"

Hetty was dressing for the outdoors too, yanking at the sleeves of her overcoat as though subduing a mortal enemy.

"Well, you're a—a fine one to tell me to calm down," she snapped at Olivia, who was so flustered she looked as though she might soon forget the whereabouts of her own head.

Outside, Alec and Blair climbed back into the buggy. Alec turned the horse down a lane that was one of Sara's favorites. Sara was in love with the countryside all around Rose Cottage and knew every nook and cranny. There was no telling where she might have gone if she wanted to hide.

"We'll have a look down this way. Come on."

Alec and Blair drove off, just passing Jasper Dale's rig as he made his way towards Rose Cottage, all unsuspecting of the tempest he was driving into. He climbed down just as Olivia burst from the house.

"Jasper!" she cried, running straight over to the buggy. Her voice sounded so full of relief Jasper clean forgot about tying up the horse.

"I, uh...brought the photographs from yesterday," he told her, fumbling under the buggy seat and feeling his ears burn pink simply at Olivia's presence. He had worked at top speed in his darkroom just to get the pictures to Olivia this morning. He would have happily toiled all night if he thought it would please her.

"Sara's run away."

"Turned out rather well..." Jasper mumbled— then stopped cold as Olivia's words sank in. From behind the little round spectacles he wore he winked owlishly and swallowed hard. "Run away?"

Olivia nodded, biting her lip.

"Her father came to take her home, and she didn't want to leave."

Olivia in distress was something Jasper had never encountered before. He clutched at the photographs, stuck them back under the buggy seat and made patting motions at Olivia.

"Just calm yourself, Olivia," he got out. "She...she can't have gone that far."

Olivia was not to be reassured, not even by a pat from Jasper Dale. She pressed her gloved hands tightly together and glanced back towards the house.

"Oh, this is all Hetty's doing. I know she's my sister, but I really don't know what to do. She'll just never change."

Even Jasper wasn't foolish enough to venture

opinions on the subject of Hetty King. Instead, his concern was for Olivia and Sara—and also for escape. In his own, less obvious way, Jasper was a man of action too.

"Well, perhaps it's time that *you* changed," he ventured, catching hold of the horse before it set out on its own. "W-well, why don't we, uh, go into town and, s-see if someone there has seen her?"

Chapter Ten

If the adults were doing a lot of running around, so were the children. At the King farm, Felicity, Felix and Andrew quietly slipped from the house and made their separate ways around to the back of the barn. No secret agents on a dangerous mission could have looked over their shoulders more often or scuttled more stealthily. In fact, they almost frightened themselves when they bumped into each other round by the barnyard fence.

Silently exchanging a look, they pulled the barn door open and quickly darted inside. When the door was shut tight, they reconnoitered the cow stalls and the feed bins and finally considered it safe to sidle over to the big old cutter, which was still shrouded in its cover.

Tapping one corner, Felicity addressed the vehicle cautiously.

"Sara," she called out, "it's just us."

The cutter remained silent. Considering herself the commanding officer of the mission, Felicity turned to her lieutenants. A good patrol was never without someone assigned to reconnaissance.

"Andrew, stay back and watch the door."

Reluctantly, Andrew stepped away and took up duty by applying one eye to a knothole in the barnboard over the door latch. Felicity addressed the cutter again, this time a little more anxiously.

"Sara?"

Still there was no answer, so Felicity grabbed the corner of the cover and whipped it back. Sara was revealed, all curled up and fast asleep under the fur rug and a blanket recently liberated from the children's bedroom.

At the flood of light, Sara twitched awake. She bumped her head on the seat side as she struggled to sit up. It was one thing to hit upon the covered cutter as the perfect hiding place. It was quite another to actually spend the night in it, trying to get comfortable on the narrow, lumpy seat and wondering what every creak and rustle was in the pitch-dark all around. It hadn't been much fun spending those long hours alone with her own thoughts and the nipping, winter cold. After much twisting and turning, Sara had just managed to doze off when her cousins arrived.

For a moment, Sara struggled to remember where she was and why she was there. Why wasn't she snuggled up in her own warm bed upstairs in Rose Cottage? Why wasn't she smelling delicious breakfast smells instead of musty hay and old fur...?

Inside of a blink it all came back, including her half-packed bags and the train tickets her father had in his pocket. Muffled in her overcoat, Sara lurched upright, stretching cramped limbs that were complaining about the sleeping quarters they had been forced to resort to.

"So, tell me all the news," she instantly ordered, looking to see if anyone had remembered to bring her some breakfast, which, of course, they had not.

Felicity could only shrug.

"Well, they're running around like ants on a griddle, and they're still at each other's throats."

Sara's face fell. She had expected her father and her Aunt Hetty to be falling all over each other by now, full of remorse and united in their frantic search. How they would hug each other with joy when Sara revealed herself to them, safe and sound and no farther away than the barn all the time. Then Sara could go into the house, get warm and get something to eat. In her rush to evade her relatives, she had forgotten entirely to bring along provisions, and her stomach was growling furiously about it.

"You mean Papa and Aunt Hetty haven't apologized yet?"

Gloomily, Felicity shook her head. She had watched everyone's behavior very closely.

"They haven't even spoken a word."

And, knowing the stubborn streak that ran in the family, they weren't likely to. Though none of the children were saying so, this looked like another of Sara's fanciful plans that wasn't going to turn out at all the way she'd expected.

"Except I heard your father say something that even I wouldn't repeat," said Felix sanctimoniously.

"What?"

This surprised even Sara, for she knew her father had to be pushed very hard to resort to swearing.

Andrew jumped back from the door.

"Quick," he warned. "Uncle Alec's coming. Hide!"

Sara dived back down under the fur rug while her cousins rolled the cover in place over the cutter. And just in time, too. Uncle Alec tramped in, banging the door behind him.

"Ah," he said, catching sight of the children, "any sign of her yet?"

As far as Alec was concerned, the children had been hunting diligently ever since he had come home with the news that Sara was missing. And such good, industrious children they were, too, making a thorough search of the barn.

Andrew shook his head, avoiding his uncle's eyes.

"No, no."

Sighing, Alec settled in against one of the upright beams supporting the hayloft. He looked just as happy to be with the young people and away from all the tension sizzling through the house. Janet was flying about in a dither of worry, Hetty was huffing and glaring, and Blair was harrying the unfortunate Constable Jeffries all around Avonlea.

"Well," he sighed, "I think I'll stay out here with you. About the only place a man can get any peace around here."

All of the children exchanged a rather panicky glance. The cover on the cutter was loose and hanging crooked, and if Sara so much as sneezed or scraped her foot inside, the game would be given away. Then how were they going to explain themselves to a collection of already furious grown-ups?

Felix, the youngest and least brave of the lot, began to look a little queasy. He liked adventures when they were fun. He didn't like them when they put him in danger of getting in hot water with his father. Shooting him a look, Felicity felt she had better say something quickly, as a diversion.

"Don't worry, Father. I'm sure Sara will turn up. How are Uncle Blair and Aunt Hetty?"

"Humph!" Alec's lip curled sardonically, expressing everything he couldn't put into words in front of the young people.

"Are they ever going to stop fighting?" Felix wondered. The sooner they stopped fighting, the sooner he could extricate himself from Sara's increasingly uncomfortable reconciliation scheme.

"Oh, probably," Alec answered dryly, "just not in our lifetime. Well, you children keep on looking, eh?"

Deciding he had better get on with the search after all, Alec changed his mind about hanging around in barn. If Janet discovered he'd been lounging about in this time of crisis, marital peace would be jeopardized for some time to come. He tramped out the way he had come, leaving the children alone again. They let out a collective breath. That had been a very close call.

"He's gone," Felicity whispered to the cutter, tugging back a corner of the old tarp.

Sara sat up, looking distinctly shaken by the narrow escape. And the news about the state of affairs between her father and her aunt had not been encouraging.

"Looks like I'm going to be here awhile. Don't forget to bring me dinner," she added, over the rumbles starting up again in her stomach. Crouching alone inside a cold, dark sleigh turned out to be a much hungrier enterprise than she had bargained for, and she was famished already.

"Don't worry," promised Felicity, turning back towards the door. If there was one thing reliable Felicity could manage for Sara, it was food.

"Bye," called Felix in Felicity's wake.

"Bye," returned Sara.

She watched the barn door creak shut behind her cousins, then, with resignation, crawled back into the cutter.

Chapter Eleven

For the rest of the day, the children made a pretense of searching the farm but, of course, did not turn up any results. Neither did the rest of the King family. Finally, late in the afternoon, Hetty, Blair, Janet and Alec gathered in the King kitchen. They all looked frazzled from their efforts and ready to burst into open hostilities on the slightest provocation. By now, they were all extremely worried, so worried that even Janet, who generally tried to keep out of King family fights, offered her own recrimination.

"Blair Stanley," she flared, "I can't help but say that if you hadn't been so dead set on leaving so quickly, none of this would have happened."

Blair got up out of his chair and went to stare out the window. He was a man used to getting things done, and he was highly frustrated by the day's lack of results. And he was not any more kindly disposed towards Hetty.

"I should have left last night, if the truth be known," he muttered darkly.

Hetty stiffened where she sat and plunked down the cup of tea she had been reviving herself with.

"If the truth be known, you should have stayed away altogether."

Blair's neck grew red just over his collar—a dangerous sign.

"It's a good job I did come back, since you seem totally incapable of keeping track of my daughter."

If Blair had wanted to enrage Hetty, he couldn't have picked a more infuriating charge than that of irresponsibility. Hetty considered herself the most dependable person in Avonlea and for many miles around.

"Just how do you intend taking care of her any better, Blair Stanley?" she demanded. "A man living on his own, preoccupied as you are with your need to conquer the business world? Why, she'll stand as much chance of living a normal life as Ruth had."

Now Hetty had truly stepped onto dangerous ground. Blair whipped around from the window so fast the curtains swayed behind him.

"What did you say?"

Drunk with the heat of battle, Hetty plunged on, right to the worst of it, the thing that had gnawed at her for years.

"Ruth would still be alive today if she hadn't fallen prey to your decadent and excessive ways."

"Hetty!" Alec cried in horror. In another minute, the two were going to come to blows.

Ignoring her brother, as though he had never spoken, Hetty continued to lambaste Blair.

"Traveling here and there, willy-nilly, picking up goodness knows what kind of diseases along the way."

Hetty was against foreign travel on principle and refused to credit any of its broadening influences. To her, it was only a dangerous frivolity bound to bring ruin upon people who might better have been staying home minding their own business. Hetty's unbridled accusation struck a pretty sore point with Blair. He grew red to the roots of his hair.

"Now you know perfectly well that Ruth contracted tuberculosis at home in Montreal," he all but shouted. "It had nothing to do with our travels. Good God, woman, when will you get that through your thick skull?"

"Now stop this, both of you!" Alec commanded, showing some steely firmness at last, lest Hetty and Blair take to yanking each other's hair out. "It's your blasted quarreling that started all this in the first place!"

"Alec!" Janet admonished sharply. After prodding Alec to take the situation in hand, she was a bit shocked when he suddenly began to. The atmosphere in the kitchen was becoming altogether too tense.

Blair stood stock-still for a moment, surprised at reprimand from Alec's direction. His jaw stood out like granite and the veins at his temple pulsed. Then, thinking better of a scorching retort, he turned towards the door.

"Well...don't expect me to stand around making pleasantries with you, Hetty. I'm going outside to look some more."

"I'll come with you," Alec said, snatching the chance to escape from the kitchen. Besides, if he went with Blair, Blair wouldn't have a chance to get annoyed with him, too. It was terrible to have these family fights going on, especially when there didn't seem to be the least thing rational about how they got started.

The turmoil among the adults had at least one positive benefit, though. It provided enough of a distracting disturbance so that Felicity, Felix and Andrew could get out the basket and slip some food into it for Sara. They might never get another chance like this, and Sara, they knew, was still hunched up in the darkened cutter, slowly starving to death.

Andrew covered the activity as best he could by standing with his back to the kitchen table while Felicity and Felix furtively stuffed leftovers from dinner under the basket lid.

"Grab some apples," Andrew whispered, just at a time, unfortunately to fall into the icy pause in conversation between the adults. Alec, who had just been on his way out behind Blair, paused mid-step. All day he had thought the children too guilty-looking and jumpy. Now he was getting a strong suspicion as to why.

"Hurry up," urged Felicity, failing to notice her father had turned away from the door and was slowly approaching from behind.

"What are you children up to?" Alec inquired quietly.

His voice, scarcely a yard away, almost gave Felicity a heart attack. Felix, never good at dissembling, thrust a jar of peaches behind his back.

"Uh...nothing," he lied shakily.

By now, everyone in the kitchen was peering at the children, and noticing the apples Felicity was about to shove into the basket. Alec pushed the lid back and looked in at what were plainly provisions for someone hiding out—someone probably named Sara.

Slowly, swallowing hard, Felicity set down the apples on the sideboard and looked up at her father. It was too late to pretend she was just planning a pleasant picnic for herself and the boys out in the freezing woods. The game was up. Alec had guessed at a glance what she was up to.

Sara, quite ignorant of the happenings in the farmhouse, was trying hard to amuse herself in the barn. Hiding inside a sleigh until a dramatic reconciliation between her nearest and dearest occurred had seemed a daring, romantic notion. In reality, it proved to be a long, excruciatingly boring wait, with no end in sight.

Sara had stayed curled up under the fur rug as long as she could stand to, but the cramped position hurt her knees abominably. On top of that, the rug turned out to have such a horsey smell that Sara began to suppose she would smell like a stable for weeks, no matter how much she scrubbed and sprinkled on eau de cologne. Besides, there was nothing to do under the dark sleigh cover but sneeze at the dust particles and listen to the barn creak in the wind.

Needless to say, for a girl of Sara's imagination and liveliness, the time began to drag past very slowly. By noon, she felt she had already spent a month twisted round in her unnatural position, with sharp bits of straw sticking into her calves. By the middle of the afternoon, it seemed more like a year.

Sara tried reciting verse to herself, tried making up a story, even tried counting sheep, but none of it did any good. She just couldn't stop thinking about her father and her Aunt Hetty, and couldn't stop being frantically curious about what might even then be happening between them. If she couldn't get up and move around she'd soon go stark raving mad!

So Sara cautiously slipped out of the sleigh, looking for amusements. She counted knotholes in the wall, swung from some hanging ropes and poked her head through a horse collar, just to try out the fit. Finally, she climbed up on a breast-high partition that divided the calf pens from the place where the hay was tossed down from the loft for the cattle. Arms outstretched, she began to walk along it as though it were a particularly challenging pasture fence, carefully placing one foot in front of the other. This was what she was in the middle of doing when Blair, Hetty, Alec, Janet, Felicity, Andrew and Felix came trooping in through the barn door.

"Sara!" Blair choked out, catching sight of his daughter first. "Thank God you're safe."

Whether she was safe or not was a moot question, for she was so startled by the intrusion that she almost lost her footing and tumbled headfirst in among the calves. Janet was, in pretty well equal parts, overjoyed and appalled to see Sara weaving precariously sideways on the narrow board holding her up. She clapped one hand to her bosom.

"Sara, oh my goodness."

Hetty, who was stiffly bringing up the rear, went papery at the sight of Sara swaying on the partition. Indeed, Hetty remained so utterly speechless that an observer might have said she was struck dumb with relief. She was struck dumb only for a moment, though. Being Hetty, she pushed her way forward, giving vent at once to all the indignation inside her. Scolding Sara was a good way to cover up how glad she really was to find the girl alive and in one piece.

"Have you any idea what you've put us through? I've a good mind to—"

"Sara, why would you do such a thing?" Blair blurted out, recovering enough to want to know and to want to cut off Hetty at the same time.

"Because she didn't want to return to Montreal with you," Hetty answered bitingly in Sara's place. "It's perfectly clear."

"What?"

This was the first time Blair had actually taken the idea seriously, and he managed to express astonishment, dismay and disbelief all in the same breath. Maybe, just maybe, there was a grain of truth to Hetty's accusations.

"It's not true, Aunt Hetty," Sara chimed in from above their heads. Couldn't any of them see that going to Montreal had become about the last thing she was worried about? While glaring at her father, Sara caught her toe and barely saved herself.

"Sara, come down from there right now!" Blair ordered.

Seeing the same old quarrel about to erupt, Sara shook her head. She moved even further out along the partition and stayed there, arms windmilling periodically to keep her upright. She had no intention of giving up the single advantage that still remained to her—the advantage of being out of reach.

"No. Why should I have to choose between Aunt Hetty and you? Mother loved you both, and so do I."

Blair turned out to be no more open to argument from Sara than from others of the family. His mouth grew very stern.

"Sara, come down now."

Sara had been prepared to hide out indefinitely in the cutter. Now she felt quite prepared to spend the rest of the week standing on top of the partition.

"Not until you've stopped quarreling. You're not being fair."

Seeing her father begin to approach, Sara realized that he would have her down in a flash if once he got within reach. In an effort to escape, Sara suddenly jumped down from the partition, luckily landing on hay ready for the cows. If her father took her into custody, she'd have no chance at all to stop the quarrel. Determined not to be caught, she scrambled backwards, not at all watching where she was going. Uncle Alec saw the danger, but he saw it too late.

"Sara, careful of that door. Sara!"

The back wall had a door set into it so that hay could be forked in from the wagons at haying time. Constructed of the same weathered boards as the rest of the barn, the door was all but invisible when closed. It was also in exactly the place Sara chose to take up her stand against the adults preparing to pursue her. She backed against it. While she was in the very act of planting her feet and glowering, the latch gave way. The door swung outward. Sara disappeared, screaming, from sight.

"Sara!" Hetty and Blair shrieked simultaneously.

Everyone stampeded over to the open door and found themselves looking down at a frightful drop created by the height of the barn's foundation and the land sloping away on that side of the barn. On the frozen ground directly below, Sara lay sprawled and motionless.

"Oh, Sara," Hetty moaned, showing more of her love for the child than at any previous, self-controlled time.

Alec, who was aware of the probable seriousness of the accident, was already heading the other way.

"I'll get the doctor," he said, doing his best to remain collected while everyone else, panic-stricken, stumbled over themselves in their rush to reach the wounded girl outside.

Chapter Twelve

If Sara wanted to create an uproar at the King farm, she certainly accomplished it by taking a tumble into the barnyard. Even as Alec struggled to harness the jittery horse to the buggy to high-tail it for the doctor, Blair was scooping Sara up in his arms, completely ignoring Hetty's frantic commands not to move her until it was known whether or not she had broken every bone in her body. Janet trotted beside Blair, feeling Sara's forehead and making small, motherly noises when Sara began to groan. Felix, Felicity and Andrew retrieved Sara's hat from where it had fallen and looked at each other in silence. They had thought up the hiding place and helped Sara to conceal herself there. With all the accusations flying back and forth, there was a good chance now that they might get blamed for the entire thing. That is, if they ever got over blaming themselves.

Hetty succeeded in badgering Blair into rushing Sara straight to her own bed in Rose Cottage. After the doctor came, there nothing anyone could do but sit in the parlor and wait—so the people in the parlor sat and waited with all their might, Alec and Hetty on one side, Jasper Dale and Olivia on the other. Jasper and Olivia had almost been run over by Alec in the village and had followed him and the doctor back, posthaste, when they heard of the catastrophe. Janet stayed at the King farm to keep an eye on the children. Blair sat upstairs with the doctor. No one could forget how pale and limp Sara had looked when she had been laid on her pillow, still unconscious, moaning raggedly.

Finally, after an age, Dr. Blair descended the stairs carrying his black bag and faced the anxious watchers in the parlor.

"Well, I've set her leg," he told them, looking just a little too grave for comfort. "It was only a small fracture. But she might have a concussion. She's sleeping quite comfortably now, but you must wake her up every hour. She must not be allowed to fall into a deep sleep."

"May I go and see her?" Olivia asked at once. Waiting helplessly in the parlor had been the worst torture she'd endured since trying to get two full sentences in a row out of Jasper Dale.

"Oh, certainly." As Olivia instantly left the room and hurried up the stairs, the doctor sighed and turned to the rest. "Well, I'll take my leave now, Hetty. Call me if there's any change at all, mmm?"

Hetty nodded, looking as though she would walk into Avonlea herself if necessary. When she got up to see the doctor to the door, he only waved her away.

"Oh, no, I'll see myself out."

"Thank you, Doctor."

As the front door closed, Alec got to his feet.

"Well, there's no point in all of us staying up all night, so, uh, I'll get back home and keep Janet and the children company. They're worried sick. Hetty..."

When Hetty looked up, Alec stopped, deciding not to broach the quarrel again. Her face was stark and drawn, and she'd clearly been through quite enough today already. Instead, Alec put his hand reassuringly on Hetty's arm.

"Goodnight," he said simply.

"Goodnight," Hetty replied, looking grateful for the silent support.

Nodding to Jasper, Alec left. With Alec gone, Jasper suddenly found himself sitting all alone in the parlor with Hetty King. For Jasper, this was just about the same as being left in a cage with a live tiger, and he began to glance nervously towards the front door through which Alec and Dr. Blair had escaped unscathed. Much as he longed to flee, though, Jasper remained heroically sitting, even with all the family tension crackling around him. Hetty or no Hetty, he was determined to wait it out for Olivia.

Upstairs, Olivia was softly pushing open the door of Sara's room. Sara, still shockingly white, was lying asleep under the quilt, her leg propped up and in a cast. Blair, who had been sitting at Sara's bedside since she had been brought in, looked up briefly as Olivia peeped in, then looked away. His face was pinched with worry and bore no sign of the belligerence that had characterized it so much with Hetty. Olivia saw that it was not a good time to go in, so she shut the door noiselessly and turned back to the corridor.

Jasper must have heard her footsteps. He leaped up like a reprieved prisoner and was already pulling on his coat when Olivia glided to the bottom of the stairs. Finding himself alone in the front hall with Olivia, speech deserted Jasper entirely.

"Oh...um..." he mumbled, wanting desperately to ask how Sara was but unable to find a single word left in his vocabulary.

Olivia, who had only caught that one distressing glimpse of the child, was on the edge of tears. She looked up at Jasper, her eyes swimming.

"Oh, Jasper...she just looks so little and...pale."

The sight of Olivia's eyes almost made Jasper's wits desert him along with his speech. He showed every sign of wanting to run or wanting to faint, and clearly had no idea what to do in such a situation. He gulped twice and, with an air of a man forcing himself through fire, laid his hand shakily on Olivia's shoulder by way of comfort.

He could have had no inkling of the effect this tiny gesture would have on Olivia. As if a spring were released, she flung both arms around Jasper's neck. The next instant, Jasper found himself hugging her to his chest and looking as

stunned as though the Avonlea Town Hall had
just tumbled down upon him.

They had forgotten all about Hetty, who was
still sitting in the parlor. Catching sight of the
tender scene, she rose to her feet as though blasted
by dynamite. She was only saved from further
action by the fact of Olivia regaining a measure of
control and letting go of Jasper. Olivia was more
than a little shocked herself at the liberty she had
just taken.

"I'm sorry," she apologized, wiping at one
eye. "The whole day's been really hard for me."

Jasper, who didn't look sorry at all, began to
twitch and bob.

"I'll...um...I'll come by tomorrow and see how
she is," he promised, his ears turning into flaming
beacons as Olivia gazed up at him.

"Thank you," returned Olivia, with more
heartfelt gratitude than Jasper could possibly
imagine he deserved.

Clutching his coat to his throat, Jasper got the
front door open. The coat remained buttoned all
lopsided, in spite of Olivia's effort to straighten it.
When Jasper left, Olivia closed the door behind
him and leaned against it for a long moment after
he was gone.

In the parlor, Hetty had sunk down again,
scandalized by the scene she had just witnessed.

Not only that, she was still holding her cup and saucer from the cup of tea she had been trying to drink. Belatedly, she tried to put them on the tea tray, only to have them tumble over the side and fall to the floor with a crash.

"Oh!" she cried in aggravation, kneeling swiftly to pick up the pieces. Why did the world have to pick today to collapse around her ears!

Startled by the clatter, Olivia pushed herself away from the door and hurried over to Hetty's side.

"Do you want some help cleaning it up?" she offered, knowing how Hetty hated any kind of mess.

How could Olivia brazenly march in like that— just after throwing herself at Jasper Dale? In irritation, Hetty took a swipe at Olivia with her napkin.

"Leave me alone, Olivia!" she snapped. "I'm perfectly capable of doing this myself!"

Being snapped at was just about the last straw for Olivia. Strengthened by her encounter with Jasper, Olivia gave vent to her own built-up exasperation.

"Hetty, you don't always have to pretend to be the strong one! If you'd only listened to me in the first place....You just end up chasing away the very people you love the most."

Olivia had failed to notice that Hetty hovered on the verge of a breakdown. To her utter astonishment, Hetty screwed up the napkin, flung it down and burst into tears.

"I know, Olivia. I know it. Now I've lost Sara. I should never have stood in Blair Stanley's way. I'm losing you, too." Hetty dabbed at her lashes and looked towards the front windows, through which Jasper Dale could be seen leaning in a dazed state against his horse. "But as you suggest, I've no one to blame but myself, so..."

Hetty snuffled loudly. Shaken thoroughly, Olivia touched a hand to her sister's shoulder. Hetty was always the firm foundation of the Kings. If Hetty crumbled, why, the whole King family would crumble too, Olivia believed.

"Hetty, you haven't lost Sara, and you haven't lost me."

Hetty turned abruptly back to the broken cup and shakily scooped up some pieces, dropping more than she picked up.

"Oh...here..." she choked, pushing a handful of china at Olivia and rushing off up the stairs herself.

Upstairs, Blair still sat holding Sara's hand as she lay asleep. Hetty opened the door and hesitated. Then, gathering all her courage, she edged inside the room. Blair looked up, but completely without hostility. With Sara in the state she was, it seemed pretty silly to be struggling over how soon she was going to get on a train. Hetty had only been acting the way she had because she, too, cared so much about Sara.

"Why don't you sit down, Hetty? There's room."

To prove it, he shifted over on the small settee and made a space for her. Awkwardly, Hetty sat down beside him just as Blair checked his watch and shook Sara gently. He was carrying out the doctor's instructions about not letting her fall into a deep sleep.

"Sara? Sara."

Sara opened her eyes the merest slit, taking in the blurry figure of her father and then—stars above—that of her Aunt Hetty!

In her bewildered condition, Sara couldn't get her eyes open any further, but her brain registered the two sworn enemies sitting meekly together, side by side on the settee. Nobody was yelling. Nobody was threatening tar or feathers, or any of the other dire menaces that had flown back and forth in the last twenty-four hours. Somehow, though Sara couldn't imagine how, her father and her Aunt Hetty had made up. Miracles must really happen after all.

Though Sara was still in some faraway world of sleep, a ghost of a smile touched her lips and she snuggled back against the pillow with a sigh. Oh yes, the end result was well worth falling backward out of a barn for.

As Sara sank back into her dreams, Hetty let out a great breath, her inflexible will unbending at last.

"Blair Stanley, like it or not, we're...bound together by...those we love."

She was thinking not only of Sara but of Ruth, whom they had all loved tremendously.

Chapter Thirteen

The day of the Avonlea skating party was everything a day for a skating party should be— brilliant, crisp, windless, and just cold enough to make a vigorous skate around the pond seem irresistibly inviting. Not only that, the much-wished-for snow had fallen, turning the fields into smooth, glittering carpets and topping the evergreens with jaunty caps of white. Into the sheds went the buggies and out came the cutters and sleighs, including the big cutter from the King barn.

Now sleighs were arriving at the pond from all

over the neighborhood. Frisky horses were stamping their feet and releasing great clouds of breath. Children were tumbling out from under sleigh rugs and racing towards the benches set up around the ice, their skates bouncing on their shoulders. People were milling on the shore and whizzing about the pond. Some did twirls and pirouettes and others gamely scraped their way back and forth, holding onto each other for support.

The King sleigh, hauled out, polished up, and hitched to the team, pulled up in the middle of all this. Alec drove. Blair, Janet, Hetty and Sara were aboard, presenting a gratifyingly united front. A firm peace treaty, or at least a lasting truce, had been hammered out between Blair and Hetty. Blair even helped Hetty down from the sleigh, making a great show of gallantry as he did so. Janet, getting out herself, lifted the rug from Sara's lap.

"Sara, how are you?" Janet inquired, a bit anxious about how Sara had managed the ride. This was really Sara's first time outside since the accident. Nothing short of total unconsciousness could have kept Sara away from the skating party.

There was no question about how Sara was. She was excited, delighted and as eager to get

over to the ice as every other child in Avonlea.
Lamentably, with her leg still in a cast, she
couldn't go anywhere without a great deal of
assistance. Her father hoisted her up effortlessly
in his arms.

"I'll take your luggage," he said to Janet with
a grin. Blair, like Sara, had been on his own too
long, and was rediscovering the joys of family
fun.

Crunching through the snow, Blair carried
Sara to a bench with a prime view of the pond.
There, he settled her comfortably, with her cast
propped up out of harm's way. When he was
done, he smiled at her fondly.

"Well, young lady, you certainly scared some
sense into your Aunt Hetty and me. Now, you
come back to Montreal whenever you're ready.
Just don't leave it too long."

Although Blair couldn't neglect his business
affairs any longer, he had been completely won
over to Sara's point of view. Blair was going back
to Montreal alone and leaving it up to Sara to
decide when she was ready to uproot herself
from Avonlea. Besides, Sara couldn't go anywhere very well until her leg was back in use
again.

Hetty bustled over with the fur rug and
tucked it solicitously around Sara. It seemed

beyond Hetty's ability to be anywhere near her niece without finding a way to fuss.

And, naturally, the Kings' arrival at the pond hadn't passed unnoticed—especially by those in Avonlea who concerned themselves with everybody's business but their own. Mrs. Potts and Mrs. Ray had arrived early, claiming to be interested in the exercise. Exchanging a significant glance, they immediately skated over to where Sara sat with her father and her aunt. They knew all about Constable Jeffries being called, of course, and the frantic search for Sara. All of it had been spiced with the most delicious rumors about fighting between Blair and Hetty, but nowhere could the two ladies glean any real details of the squabble. Now, if they poked in just the right spot, some juicy information might shake loose.

"Why, Blair Stanley," Mrs. Potts twittered in that fake, sugary tone guaranteed to set a person's teeth on edge. "Isn't it wonderful how nothing was proven against you? I must say, we've followed your case with such interest."

When she wanted to, Mrs. Potts had a way of saying things that could make even an angel seem black with guilt. Hetty's mouth grew prunish.

"Of course you have, Clara Potts," Hetty

rasped, deliberately diverting the woman away from Blair.

"Good day to you," Mrs. Potts said, forced to acknowledge Hetty, with whom she was not on the best of terms. The two had exchanged words before, none of them to Clara Potts's advantage.

"Good day," added Mrs. Ray, in grudging support of her companion.

Blair, far from being annoyed by their insinuations, doffed his hat with exaggerated courtesy and favored both women with an impudent grin.

"Good day to you, ladies," he returned pleasantly, not even bothering to disguise the irony in his voice.

Transfixed by Hetty's stare and Blair's brash good humor, the two women realized they had come to the wrong place to fish for a scandal. Faces stiff, Mrs. Ray and Mrs. Potts backed up and lumbered away across the ice. They could hardly wait to get out of earshot to break into sniffs of censure and disparagement.

After the two women had vanished into the swirling crowd, Sara looked up at her father. There was a twinkle in her eye.

"I said all the people in Avonlea were interesting, Papa. I didn't say they were all nice."

Hetty, pleased at the rout of her old antagonists, turned to tug the rug over Sara's knees.

"Now, you keep yourself covered there, Sara. We don't want you catching pneumonia on top of all this."

Hetty was getting back to her old form, seeing a calamity behind every bush. Sara smiled back at her affectionately, then spotted Felicity and Cecily, who had come earlier with Olivia, chasing each other merrily among the other children.

Then, amazingly, a long, thin figure appeared on the pond, legs rubbery, arms flapping, skates slipping and sliding in a desperate effort to keep the wearer upright. The figure was Jasper Dale, twice as ridiculous on ice as he was on dry land, yet bravely daring to appear before all of Avonlea. Such a sight hadn't been seen within living memory, and everyone stared as Jasper tilted sideways, skidded in a half-circle, caught his heel and finally fell into a heap right at Sara's feet.

"Oh, hello, Sara Stanley," he said cheerfully from an inch above the ice. A year ago, Jasper would have died of mortification at making such a spectacle of himself. Now, Sara and Olivia had given him the courage to fall down and not mind a bit.

"Hello, Mr. Dale," Sara smiled. She was used to Jasper's ways and hardly blinked when he collapsed beside her.

By dint of great effort, Jasper got himself to his elbows and brushed some of the snow off his clothes.

"So, how's the, uh, leg?"

"Oh, much better, thank you."

Now Hetty finally appeared to notice the man who was sprawled before her. If anyone had looked at her closely, they might even have suspected a glimmer of tolerance in her eye.

"Jasper," she said, with less than her usual asperity. "This is a surprise. When was the last time you attended the, uh, Avonlea skating party?"

A word from Hetty, and Jasper was thrown into confusion again.

"Oh, well, I haven't been s-s-sk—"

"Skating," Hetty supplied, thinking Jasper might strangle on the spot if she waited for him to get the word out himself.

"—skating in a dog's age. I just came to see Sara."

This fooled no one, least of all Hetty.

"And Olivia, too, no doubt," Hetty added. "Well, she's over there."

With an air of making a great concession, Hetty pointed to Olivia, who was halfway across the pond, talking to some of her friends. At the same moment, Olivia spotted Jasper struggling to get up. She immediately laughed and beckoned him to come over.

For Jasper, this was a major challenge, but he faced it stalwartly. Rising from the ice, he stood teetering on the thin, silver blades of his skates.

"Bye," he said to Sara and her party.

Without falling once, Jasper wobbled all the way over to Olivia and offered his arm. Olivia grasped it firmly, doing her best to provide a firm support for Jasper without in the least appearing to. Swaying precariously, they skated away, with Hetty watching every movement.

"Sara, will you look at that?" she sniffed. "I must say, Olivia's quite forward, taking his arm like that. Hmm, you'd almost think they were courting."

"I think they are courting, Aunt Hetty," Sara replied sagely and with high humor.

"What?"

But before Hetty could provide any prickly opinions regarding Jasper Dale, Alec arrived. He held out his hand for Hetty to join him. Alec was feeling jovial, as any man would after the way the family disagreements had worked themselves out.

"Come on, Hetty, don't be an old stick in the mud."

"I, I don't skate," Hetty shot back in alarm, for Alec, she saw, was in a reckless mood.

"It's never to late to learn. Come on, you don't need skates when you're with me."

Before Hetty could resist, Alec had her by the arm and up on the ice. Ignoring her squawks, he swung her round on the slick surface, laughing heartily. Though no youngster, Alec was a lot like Felix. He still liked a chance to tease his older sister.

"Aunt Hetty had better watch out," cried Sara, as Hetty executed a skidding arc, her skirts flying out behind her. "She's liable to break her own leg."

Hetty was a sight indeed, trying madly to hang onto her dignity in front of all Avonlea while at the same time hissing fiercely under her breath for Alec to stop. Grinning at her, Alec continued to swing Hetty until he got so carried away he hit a patch of rough ice with his foot and lost his grip completely.

Sara's mouth popped open as she saw her Aunt Hetty whirl around one more time on her own momentum, her high-booted feet frantically scrabbling under her. Her boots got no purchase at all on the ice. The next thing Sara knew, Hetty was seated flat on her behind, skidding sideways halfway across the pond on her bottom, coming to rest not a yard away from Olivia and Jasper and Mrs. Potts. Her skirts were tangled up around her knees, her hat was hanging off over one ear, and her expression would have frightened a crocodile.

In an instant, a crowd of other skaters closed around Hetty, helping her to her feet and roaring with laughter. Even Sara gave way to a fit of giggles, especially seeing how sheepish her Uncle Alec looked, and how quickly he took to his skates as soon as Hetty's ruffled figure pushed through the ring of spectators, searching for him.

Blair, also very guilty of enjoying Hetty's tumble, turned to Sara.

"May your father have the honor of skating with you?"

"How?" asked Sara incredulously. With her leg in a cast, she couldn't even shift from the bench.

"Ah, like this!"

Lightly, Blair picked Sara up and deposited her in the little wooden sleigh he had provided as a special surprise for his daughter. It was painted bright red, with slender runners, and a high, curved handle behind.

"Gently...yes," Blair assured her.

With an ease and grace that outdid everyone

else on the pond, Blair got behind the sled and pushed Sara almost magically over the ice.

"All right, you're in control," he laughed, weaving right and left just as Sara directed.

Beaming, Sara made sure he pushed her past every one of her friends and everyone who had ever tried to taunt her. She did have a father, a handsome—innocent father—and she wanted everyone to see how terribly proud of him she was.

The crowd opened readily for the sled, shouting and waving as Sara flew by. Sara waved back, ecstatic at having her father by her side, the familiar people of Avonlea around her, and her Aunt Hetty, brushed off and restored to good temper by Uncle Alec, actually smiling at Blair. Sara didn't know what the future held and, for the moment, didn't care. She was taking her life one day at a time—and today was absolutely perfect.

❧   ❧   ❧